Liar, Liar

Barthe DeClements

MARSHALL CAVENDISH
New York

I wish to thank Susan Brown and her students for their contributions
to this story. I wish to thank Jacquelyn Hallquist, my daughter,
Nicole Southard, and my grandson, Scott Southard, for their work on
the manuscript and to thank Sharyn November for lending me her
melodious name.
B.D.

Library of Congress Cataloging-in-Publication Data
DeClements, Barthe.
Liar, liar / written by Barthe DeClements. — 1st ed.
p.   cm.
Summary: Sixth-grader Gretchen and her friends begin to have problems when
a new girl starts telling some very believable, but untrue, stories.
ISBN 0-7614-5021-1
[1. Honesty—Fiction. 2. Schools—Fiction. 3. Friendship—Fiction.
4. Family life—Fiction.] I. Title.
PZ7.D3584L1   1998   [Fic}—dc21   97-17716   CIP   AC

The text of this book is set in 12.5 point Berkeley Oldstyle Book

Book design by Constance Ftera

Printed in the United States of America

3   5   6   4   2

*This book is dedicated
to my friend, Josie Reyes*

Contents

CHAPTER 1

Close Shave

❦ Everything had been easy until sixth grade. That was when Marybelle moved into our neighborhood. Until then, we were a nice class. Got along fine with each other. Except when Spider Black yelled at me during baseball games, "Come on! Knock it out of the field, Grizzy!"

I could knock it out of the field, but I'd turn and yell at him, "I'll knock it through teeth, *Harlan*."

"Grizzy, Grizzy, Grizzy! We need a homer," he'd sing back.

It was no use.

On my weekends with Mom, I asked her, "Instead of taking your husbands' names, why didn't you stick with your own name? Jones is fine. Gretchen Jones would be cool. Who wants to be called Gretchen Griswald? Do you know that Spider Black calls me Grizzy? How would you like to be called Grizzy?"

"I wouldn't like to be called Spider," Mom said.

"Spider" Harlan Black didn't mind. Who'd like to be called Harlan?

At home with Dad, when I was supposed to be doing my homework, I'd scribble "Gretchen Black" on the cover of my notebook. Then I'd erase it.

I wasn't the only girl who liked Spider. My best friend, Susan November, once admitted to me that she did. She has such a neat name. Susan November.

And pretty hair, too. Reddish blond. Thick. Very thick and curly. She makes a big fuss when she combs it. "I just can't get a comb through it," she complains.

Tough. How'd she like boring brown hair?

"But your hair is so shiny," she says.

That's something, at least.

But I thought Susan was great. And I liked everyone in our class. Our only problem was hyperactive Robbie, and even he was okay if he took his medicine. Our class was so nice that in sixth grade we were given to Ms. Cooper, who was a first-year teacher.

Ms. Cooper tried to make our lessons interesting. We studied U.S. history and built log cabins out of clay. The clay zoomed around the room a bit. Ms. Cooper wasn't much on discipline. But we settled down when the teacher next door stuck his head in our room.

Then Marybelle moved to our neighborhood in Everett, Washington. She had green eyes and small white teeth and a cute turned-up nose. I pushed up my nose and peered into the bathroom mirror. Disgusting. "Oink," I said to myself.

One morning, I was sitting on top of Crystal's desk. We always sat on each others' desks and raked over the TV shows until three minutes after the last bell rang and Ms. Cooper was frantically flapping her gradebook.

The bell hadn't even rung this morning when Marybelle shoved a grocery sack at my chest. "Look inside," she ordered.

Instead, I looked at her. Her small white teeth glistened. Her green eyes glittered.

I leaned away. "What've you got?"

"Look inside, dummy."

I looked in the sack. "A towel and a shaver?"

"That's an electric hair trimmer. It's for my demonstration talk," Marybelle explained.

I shoved the sack back at her. "You're not demonstrating on me."

"Me, either," Crystal said.

"But I have to demonstrate on somebody," Marybelle said and took the sack to her seat.

We had Language Arts after lunch recess. Everyone was sleepy and sweaty. Ms. Cooper said that we'd be finishing up the last of the demonstration talks. She called on Arnold first.

He's a science brain and his talk was on black holes. He demonstrated them by pushing globs of astral matter through a swirling hole on a hunk of black cardboard.

I watched him with my chin on my hand and my eyes half closed.

"Marybelle, we'll have you next," Ms. Cooper said when Arnold was finished.

Marybelle went to the front of the room carrying her sack. She said to Ms. Cooper, "I'll need a helper."

Ms. Cooper nodded. "Choose anyone you would like to help you."

Marybelle licked her lower lip with her tongue while she surveyed our room. "Um, a . . . Susan."

Susan came up and stood beside Marybelle.

Marybelle pulled the stool away from the whiteboard. "You'll have to sit on this. Face the class."

Susan got on the stool and faced us. Marybelle draped the towel around her neck and plugged the hair trimmer into the wall socket. When Susan heard the whir of the trimmer, her shoulders straightened and her eyes widened. "You're not going to —"

Marybelle raised a hand to quiet Susan while she gave us the phony smile of a TV pitchwoman. "Today I'm going to demonstrate the advantages of trimming your hair at home. A trim in a beauty parlor or barber shop costs between ten dollars and forty dollars. This efficient home trimmer costs only eight dollars and ninety-five cents and has a three-year guarantee. As you can see, it's light and flexible."

Marybelle held the trimmer high and turned her wrist this way and that.

"When giving a home trim, the first thing to do is take two inches of hair between your first and second fingers." Marybelle shoved her fingers into a thick clump of Susan's hair and pulled up.

Susan cringed. "Oww!"

"You really should have your hair thinned, dear," Marybelle said. Then she zipped the trimmer over the top of Susan's head.

Susan jerked away to peer at the floor. "You better not cut any off."

Marybelle gave her a professional pat on the shoulder. "This is just a demonstration, dear."

About this time, Robbie began to hop around in his seat. I noticed before Ms. Cooper did. She was dutifully taking notes on Marybelle's clearness of delivery, poise, and posture.

Marybelle pretended to finish the top of Susan's hair, picking up clumps, one after another, and zipping the trimmer in the air.

This was getting boring. I looked at Robbie again. He was shooting at a phantom airplane that seemed to be flying about six feet in front of him.

"When you finish with the top," Marybelle told us, "you trim up the sides and the back. And *then* . . ." Big pause. She was losing her audience and knew she had to get some drama into her performance.

She'd lost Ms. Cooper completely. Robbie was out of his seat and kneeling in the aisle to get better shots at his plane. Ms. Cooper pulled him to his feet and whispered something in his ear. She probably was asking him if he'd taken his pills.

"Now that the hair is trimmed, you can carve designs in it. Some guys like stripes on the sides. I, personally, like a stripe up the back." Marybelle leaned down to Susan. "What do you like, dear?"

Susan shrugged. "Oh, the side."

Marybelle pointed her trimmer at the side of Susan's head and zoomed in. Fluffs of blond hair tumbled over the trimmer and onto the floor.

My mouth dropped open.

"Whoa!" somebody yelled from the back of the room.

But Marybelle plowed right up to the top of Susan's head before she lifted the trimmer.

Susan clapped her hand to the bare strip. Her eyes bugged at the curls on the floor and then at Marybelle. "What did you do to me?" she screamed.

Susan jumped off the stool, ran to the sink, and stared horrified into the mirror, whimpering, "Oh, no. Oh, no."

Ms. Cooper had been settling Robbie into his chair. She held him by the shoulder while she looked from Susan to Marybelle. What had happened didn't seem to be registering in her brain.

"What . . . ? What did you do?" she asked Marybelle.

Marybelle was busy pulling the plug out of the wall socket. "I guess the trimmer must have slipped," she murmured.

14

Ms. Cooper slowly let go of Robbie. Slowly she made it to the classroom sink, picking up one foot after the other as though she were wading through floodwaters.

"Here," she said to Susan, who was sobbing by now, "I think you could just brush your hair over the little spot."

Ms. Cooper tried desperately to claw lumps of Susan's hair across the two-inch naked path that ran up the side of her head. Every time a curl stubbornly sprang back into its place, Ms. Cooper's face grew a pukier shade of yellow.

I was thinking it was lucky she was at the sink.

"Maybe for this afternoon you could just wear my head scarf." Ms. Cooper tried to give Susan a cheery smile, but Susan wasn't buying it.

She wiped her runny nose across her arm and announced, "I'm going home to tell my mother!"

CHAPTER 2

Deep Trouble

🍎 "No, no, Susan." Ms. Cooper shook her head. "You can't leave the school grounds. You have to have permission from the office and your parents for that."

Susan kept on sniffling and dragging her jacket off a clothes hook. "My mom works at home. I'll call her from the office phone."

Ms. Cooper opened and closed her mouth like a guppy. She seemed to think a minute. Then she went to the intercom and announced to the office secretary that Susan November would be down to call her mother.

After Ms. Cooper hung up, she said, "I'm very sorry an accident happened to your hair, Susan."

"It wasn't an accident," Susan said and went out the classroom door.

There were three kids who still hadn't given their talks, but I guess Ms. Cooper wasn't up to more demonstrations. She told us to take out our library books. While we read, she sat at her desk and stared out the window.

I sat in my seat and thought of the deep trouble that Ms. Cooper was in. Maybe she didn't know Susan's mom yet, but I did. Mrs. November isn't a person you want to mess with. She's the kind of parent who expects her kids to get straight A's. If they don't, she's down at the school to find out why.

Mrs. November always volunteers for field trips. And all the kids try to wiggle out of being in her group. They want to ride with the parents who hunch over their steering wheels with smiles pasted on their faces while the kids belt out "One Hundred Bottles of Beer on the Wall" and wave their hands out the windows.

If you ride with Mrs. November, she marches you to her van and won't start the motor until each seat belt is fastened and everyone is sitting up straight. If any kid gets out of order, she pulls the van to the side of the road.

Mrs. November does one good thing. She buys Susan the coolest clothes in the class. I think she knows how because she's an interior decorator.

It isn't much fun being in their gorgeous house, though. You can't touch anything that belongs to Mrs. November. If you do, she or Susan's sister, Lindsi, will tell you to put it down. Also, you're not supposed to make any noise when Mrs. November's talking on the phone, and she's always getting business calls.

I keep my mouth shut around her, but I didn't know what poor Ms. Cooper would do.

When the school bell rang, all the kids clapped their

books closed and put them in their desks. Ms. Cooper told us we were dismissed. We didn't even have to pick up the junk on the floor before we left.

Out at the buses, Marybelle tried to laugh off "the accident."

"A nick would have been an accident," I told her. "Shaving half of Susan's head wasn't an accident."

Even though Marybelle's stop is next to mine, I took a seat in the back with Crystal and Masaka. After all, Susan was my best friend.

I called her as soon as I got home. I didn't get an answer until five o'clock. "Where have you been?" I asked her.

"At the hair salon," Susan said.

"Did they fix everything?"

"How can you *fix* a bald spot?" Susan asked.

"I don't know. Cut the rest of your hair short?"

"They did that. But I still look like I have a disease. What did Ms. Cooper do to Marybelle?"

"Nothing. Marybelle told her it was an accident and Ms. Cooper didn't see Marybelle shave you, so she couldn't yell at her."

"Ms. Cooper saw my bare head."

"I know," I said. "I think she felt bad. Are you coming to school tomorrow?"

"Me and my *mother*."

I shivered. "Ohhh, poor Ms. Cooper."

"She deserves everything she gets. She should have

punished Marybelle." Susan sounded really bitter. I wondered how mad her mother was.

At dinner I told Dad about the whole thing. "What do you think Mrs. November will do?" I asked him.

"She'll probably have Ms. Cooper's job," he said.

"What would you do if Marybelle did it to me?" I wondered.

"I'd shave off the rest of your hair, get you some gigs as a folksinger, and retire."

I pulled my fork through the cheesy lasagna on my plate. "Wouldn't you even tell the principal on Ms. Cooper?"

"Sounds to me," Dad said, "as if Ms. Cooper has enough punishment with Marybelle in her class."

"Marybelle's just a regular kid," I said.

"Maybe," Dad said.

I would have asked him what he meant by that, but the phone rang. It was Mom. She wanted to know if Dad could take my brothers this weekend instead of the next.

"Have them bring their bikes," Dad told her, "and we'll go trail riding."

Dad tries to plan an outdoor activity on my brothers' visits. That's easier than having them inside the house. During the divorce, Mom made a big deal about getting custody of her kids, but she doesn't spend much time training the boys.

Jimmy, my real brother, is only eight and he's usually quiet. My two half-brothers, Jason and Keith, are wild.

They're thirteen and fifteen. When Dad gets a chance, he tries to be a decent father to them. Role model, he says. Their own dad, Mom's first husband, is an alcoholic.

Maybe it seems strange for the mother to have custody of the sons and the father to have the daughter, but Dad wouldn't let Mom have both Jimmy and me. I chose to stay with him because if I lived in Mom's house, I'd be spending all my time cleaning up after my brothers.

Dad's and my place isn't a magazine spread like the Novembers', but it's neat and comfortable. Mom's is a total wreck. Since she's a computer programmer, you'd think she'd have her life organized. I love her, but I have to admit she isn't much of a housekeeper.

"How come Mom wants the boys to stay here this weekend?" I asked Dad when he was off the phone.

"She says she has a chance to fly to Reno," he said.

"I hope she isn't going to get married again."

Dad shrugged. "She's a pretty woman."

"How come you two got married anyway?"

Dad shrugged again. "She's a pretty woman."

"That's a stupid reason to get married," I told him.

"So. You're only going to do intelligent things when you grow up?" Dad took his empty plate to the sink, rinsed it off, and put it in the dishwasher. Then he turned around and looked back at me. "Who's the *cutest* boy in your classroom? And how many of you girls like him best?"

"That doesn't count," I said. "I'm only twelve. You're supposed to be smarter when you're older."

Dad laughed all the way to the living room.

On the bus the next morning, I could hardly wait to see Susan. "Maybe she'll wear a cap," Crystal said.

I was on the window side, so I peered out when we pulled up to her stop. "She isn't wearing a cap," I said. "She's wearing a purple headband.

"Your haircut looks cool," Crystal told Susan when she dropped into the seat in front of us. "That was a smart idea to wear a headband."

Susan turned around to face us. "It was my mom's idea. She bought me three different colors."

Marybelle leaned across the aisle. "Susan, you look like Madonna."

Susan totally ignored her. And Susan kept on ignoring her when we got off the bus, even though Marybelle trotted along beside us on the way to our classroom.

Mr. Swenson, the principal, was in the room when we got there. He was talking to Ms. Cooper. The only thing I heard him say was something about the music period.

While we hung up our jackets, I whispered to Susan, "When's your mom coming to school?"

"She has a conference with the principal at ten-thirty."

That was when we had our music period.

"Your mom's coming to school?" Spider asked Susan.

"Of course," she said.

Spider grinned at Marybelle. "What do you want on your tombstone?"

"It was an *accident!*" Marybelle insisted.

Spider nodded, still grinning.

The last bell rang, and we moved toward our desks because the principal was there.

He turned from Ms. Cooper and watched us with a stern look on his face. He waited, not saying anything. Kids started poking each other and hissing, "Shhh!"

Mr. Swenson still waited with that stern look on his face. When we were all quiet, he asked, "What does the eight-thirty bell mean?"

No one raised a hand, so he called on Amy.

Amy said, "It means you're supposed to get in your seat and be quiet."

"No, it doesn't." Mr. Swenson pointed at Arnold. "Arnold, what does the eight-thirty bell mean?"

"It signals the start of classes," Arnold said.

"Exactly! It signals the moment your lessons begin."

I was thinking that roll had to be taken before the lessons could begin, but I didn't make a peep.

"The next time I visit your room in the morning, I expect you to be in your seats ready to work when the eight-thirty bell rings." Mr. Swenson nodded to Ms. Cooper and left the room.

I guessed we weren't the nicest class in the school anymore.

CHAPTER 3

No Brother of Mine

❦ When ten-thirty came, Ms. Cooper told us to line up to go to the music room. We milled around the door in our easygoing way.

"Straighten up your line and be quiet!" she snapped.

We straightened up.

"I don't want to hear a word out of any of you when we're in the halls. All right, march!"

Robbie gave her a salute and led us in a military march down the hall to the music room. Out of the corner of my eye, I watched Ms. Cooper hurry to the office. There were brown circles under her eyes, and she looked thin and small in her navy blue dress. She usually wore pants and bright-colored sweaters. I hadn't seen her in a dress since the first day of school.

Mr. Monte, the music teacher, was standing in front of his podium. He looked over his glasses at us as we took our places in the stands. "My, you're a silent bunch today. Have you been bad?"

"One of us spoiled everything," Arnold said.

We all stared at Marybelle. She flipped her hands over and shrugged her shoulders. She wasn't about to take any blame.

Susan pulled back her headband to reveal the bald strip. "Look at my hair!"

Mr. Monte leaned forward. "Hmmm. Well, I guess we'd better sing a song for you. How about 'Casey Would Waltz with the Strawberry Blond'?"

I love that song. And I love Mr. Monte. He's a human-being teacher.

When we got back to our classroom, Spider was still humming. He stopped when he saw Ms. Cooper frowning from her desk.

We took our seats and sat as quietly as mice.

The secretary's voice boomed over the intercom. "Ms. Cooper, will you please send Marybelle Jackson to the office."

"Yes," Ms. Cooper said. "Marybelle, will you please go to the office."

We all watched her walk to the classroom door. She wasn't flipping her hands around now. She looked really nervous. I'd have been scared to death.

Crystal sits in front of me. She turned her head to whisper, "Maybe she'll get suspended."

"Crystal!" Ms. Cooper has a thin voice to go with her thin body, but it cut across the room. Crystal whipped her head around.

"There's to be no talking in here," Ms. Cooper ordered. "Take out your math books and turn to page thirty-seven."

Story problems. I hate story problems.

Marybelle came back just before lunch. She was carrying a white envelope, but she didn't look sad.

At lunchtime we eat in our classroom, and we get to move our chairs around. Crystal and I scooted over to Marybelle's desk to find out what happened to her.

"Did you have to see the principal?" Crystal asked.

"Sure." Marybelle took a brown banana from her lunch sack and began to peel it.

I hate rotten bananas. They stink.

Crystal poked Marybelle in the arm. "And so?"

"He just asked me what happened and I told him. Then he asked me if I thought a hair trimmer was an appropriate thing to bring to school." Marybelle had bitten off a hunk of the banana and was talking through the gooey lumps in her mouth. "I told Mr. Swenson that Eric had done his demonstration with his dad's fly rod, and it had real fish hooks in it."

Marybelle stopped a second to swallow. "Then he asked if my parents knew I brought the hair trimmer to school. Maybe he didn't believe me when I said they did because he tried to call my house. Nobody was there, so I have to take a letter home and have my parents sign it."

"Is that all he's going to do to you?" I couldn't believe her luck.

I told my dad Marybelle hadn't gotten in much trouble and neither had Ms. Cooper, as far as I could tell.

"They're not going to tell you." Dad's a personnel director and knows about these things. "My guess is that the incident has been written up in your teacher's file, and the principal will keep an eye on her."

"That isn't much," I said.

"Well, I don't think a first-year teacher would be happy to have an official complaint from a parent."

"It's just making her crabby," I said. "She never used to be crabby."

It turned out Dad was right about the principal keeping an eye on Ms. Cooper. Mr. Swenson popped in on us every day and sometimes twice. He was there Friday morning when we were taking our spelling test. Ms. Cooper was dictating the words and we were writing them down. Mr. Swenson walked around the room and then went out the door.

We had a *National Geographic* film during our last period. Afterwards, Ms. Cooper told us to clean up around our desks. She unplugged the TV and wound up the cord. Katie took the wastebasket up and down the aisles so we could dump our junk in it.

Spider and Eric made airplanes out of their used paper. When Katie started down their aisle, they flew their airplanes toward the basket. Robbie saw them and stood on his seat to shoot a crumpled wad of paper.

That's when Mr. Swenson came in our room again.

Ms. Cooper was pushing the TV cart towards the door to put it in the hall, and she almost ran into him.

She took a quick look at Mr. Swenson and then at us. This time her face turned bright pink.

"Robbie, sit down!" she commanded.

"Well, Spider and Eric were . . ." Robbie tried to explain, but Ms. Cooper cut him off.

"Sit down!"

"You don't have to yell," he mumbled and sat down.

Mr. Swenson moved to the front of the room. "I have always been proud of this class. And now you are disappointing me, your teacher, and your school. Put your heads on your desks and think about this until the bell rings."

I put my head on my desk and heard the TV cart roll and the faint sound of Mr. Swenson and Ms. Cooper talking in the hall. I wondered if he were blaming her.

"Why don't you give that teacher a break and behave?" Dad asked me that night when I told him what happened.

"Kids always make paper airplanes and shoot them at the wastebasket if no one's watching," I said. "It isn't evil."

Dad didn't argue with me. We were making a lunch for our bike trip up the Centennial Trail the next day. "Chicken sandwiches or tuna?" He held up two cans.

"Both," I said. "You know Keith and Jason."

The boys eat like Mom hasn't fed them for a month.

They were barely in the house the next morning when they hit the refrigerator. We'd packed the bottles of raspberry soda so there was only milk to drink. Keith took out the carton and gurgled down the whole thing.

"Hey, save some for me," Jason said.

Keith tossed him the empty carton and headed for the lunch basket, which was on the washing machine. "What's in there? Any cookies?"

"Leave that alone," I told him. "We're taking it with us."

Luckily, Dad, Mom, and Jimmy came in the kitchen then. Jimmy gave me a bear hug and Mom kissed me.

She told me I was getting taller and prettier. Her head was tilted to the side and her eyes were swimmy as she looked me over. "I'll bring you back a cashmere sweater if I win, lovey."

"Just bring me smackeroos," Keith told her.

"Me, too," Jason said.

"What do you want?" she asked Jimmy.

"I'll take smackeroos," he said.

A car honked outside.

"I've got to go," Mom said. "We can't miss the plane. You boys be good."

"Aren't we always?" Keith asked.

She gave Jimmy a pat on the head and hurried out of the kitchen.

After she was gone, the boys loaded our bikes into the back of Dad's truck and then climbed in. I sat in the front with the lunch basket on my lap. As Dad left Everett and drove across the trestle to Machias, I wondered who was going to Reno with Mom. It could be a woman friend, but I guessed it was a man.

The boys would know. And Dad probably saw the car when Mom was coming in the house. I didn't think it was something I should ask about. I never did know who wanted the divorce, Dad or Mom.

I was only eight at the time. Jimmy's age. But I knew even then that Mom liked adventures and Dad ate poached eggs on toast every morning of the year.

"Great day for a bike ride," Dad said. "We're lucky to have a warm February."

"Yes," I said, "and in June when school is out, it'll rain."

"Well, that's the Northwest. Hand me my sunglasses. They're in the glove compartment."

I handed them to him. He put them on and looked just like a movie star. Except for the bald circle on the back of his head.

In Machias, we passed the fire station. A red engine was sitting outside the old-fashioned building. From the bed of our truck came the sound of a siren. *Woooowowowowo.* I looked through the back window to see Keith and Jason with their mouths in the air like a pair of wolves.

Dad pulled the truck into a parking space at the beginning of the trail. He was disgusted when he found out that Keith and Jason had forgotten their helmets. Dad made Jason wear his.

Jason hated that. He's kind of a wannabe. He wants to be tough, but he's skinny and weak. Not burly like Keith.

Keith hit the trail first. Then Jason. Then me. Dad had to hitch the basket to his rear fender, so he and Jimmy trailed a half mile behind us.

There were horses and skaters and walkers on the trail. Keith rode in and out of them, steering with his knees. Jason wanted to be just as cool, so he took his hands off his handlebars. He turned around to see if I was watching, and plowed smack into a baby buggy.

The buggy didn't flip, but Jason did. When I rode by, the baby's mother was standing over him, telling him what a stupid, careless, idiot boy he was. I kept right on going as if he were no brother of mine.

At the park in Snohomish, Keith and I climbed down the bank to the Pilchuk River. While we ate our sandwiches and drank our sodas, I told Keith about Marybelle shaving Susan's hair and saying it was an accident.

"We had a guy on our wrestling team who was like that," Keith said. "He'd do anything to win. When he got called on a violation, he'd claim he didn't know his move was illegal."

I tossed a piece of crust toward two mallards that were swimming down the river. "What did you do when that guy tried something illegal on you?"

Keith shrugged. "Nothing. Just ignored him."

"Ignored him?"

"Sure. Liars trap themselves in their own webs. Eventually the coach caught on and cut the guy from the team."

"Nothing's happened to Marybelle," I said.

"Yet," Keith said.

Jason came scrambling down the rocks to us. "Man, it's hot out. I'm sweating."

"No problem," Keith told him. "I'll help you. Gimmie your soda a minute."

Stupid Jason handed him the bottle.

Keith put his finger over the top, shook the bottle, and pointed it at Jason's head. Sticky raspberry soda sprayed all over Jason's face and hair.

Jason tried to wipe it off with the end of his T-shirt. "I'm going to get you, Keith," he said. "I'm going to get you in your bed some night."

Dad yelled at us to come up for dessert.

Dessert was giant oatmeal cookies. Jason only took two bites before he was pawing through the lunch basket. All he stirred up were empty bottles and sandwich wrappings.

He turned to Dad, who was sitting on a log with Jimmy. "Isn't there anything else to drink?" Jason asked him.

"No," Dad said. "I brought a bottle for each of us."

"Ya, but Keith spilled mine." He eyed Jimmy, whose bottle was half full. "Here, Jimmy, I'll help you."

"No, you don't!" Jimmy put the bottle behind his back.

"We'll stop at the store on the way home to pick up more milk," Dad said.

"But we have to ride six miles to the car and I'm thirsty!" Jason complained.

Dad said he was sorry, but he couldn't do anything about that. Jason stamped over to his bike and sat down on the ground to sulk until we were ready to leave.

I felt a little sorry for him on the bike ride back. His face dripped with sweat under Dad's helmet, and he'd been called an idiot and sprayed with soda. He was such a baby, though.

CHAPTER 4

Smackeroos

❦ Sunday morning we took the bikes out again and rode down to the Everett Community College campus. It's a safe place to practice wheelies. When we got home, Dad and Jimmy made chili and Keith and Jason fought over the TV.

Keith spotted Jason going for the remote control on the coffee table. He jumped in Jason's path. Jason tried to plow through him, but Keith planted his hand on Jason's forehead to keep him at arm's length. Jason batted at Keith, but he was too short to reach him. Keith just stood there holding Jason off and laughing at him.

When this got boring, Keith shoved Jason backwards and snatched the remote control. Jason raised his leg to give Keith a kick in the shins. He shouldn't have tried that. It gave Keith a chance to grab Jason's foot, drop him to the floor, and clamp him in a headlock.

Jason grunted and squirmed in Keith's grip, trying to grab Keith's hair.

"Forget it," Keith said and squeezed Jason's head until tears sprang from his eyes.

By this time, I was standing on the couch so I wouldn't get hit by flying feet. The commotion must have drifted into the kitchen, because Dad appeared in the doorway.

"You boys get up right now," he ordered.

They untangled themselves and stood up.

"Go on outside and split wood," Dad told them. "Make yourselves useful for a change."

I don't know if I'd let them near an axe, but they weren't my problem. I went in my room and read *Julie of the Wolves*. I wish I had a wolf.

Mom didn't come for the boys until ten-thirty. Poor Jimmy could hardly keep his eyes open while he waited for her. I was almost asleep in the rocking chair.

She burst in the front door like a swirling wind, waving a package in one hand and a white cloth bag in the other. "I won! I won! I won *big*!"

"Here, Lovey!" She tossed me the package and then cuddled into the rocking chair with me.

"Open it! Open it!"

I opened the box and pulled away the tissue paper. "Oh, that's beautiful!" I stroked the velvety soft, chocolate-colored sweater.

"It matches your great big, beautiful eyes." Mom scrunched my cheeks with her long fingers and gave me a kiss on my mouth.

"What about us?" Jason was looking like he might cry. "Didn't you bring anything for us?"

"Smackeroos. You said you wanted smackeroos." She picked up the bag she'd dropped on the floor and went over to Jimmy. "You first, because you're the littlest."

She untied the string that was around the neck of the bag, scooped out silver dollars, and counted eight of them into his cupped hands. "Gee, thanks," he said.

"And you get thirteen because you're thirteen," she told Jason.

Jason stuffed the coins into the pockets of his jeans. Keith did the same with his fifteen dollars.

Mom threw me the bag. "Here, lovey, you get the rest."

I caught the bag, but I didn't open it, because Jason was watching me. I didn't want to take the chance that I got more dollars than he did.

"What was Reno like?" Keith asked Mom.

She told us about the sparkling lights and games and slot machines until Jimmy keeled over onto Keith, fast asleep.

"You better finish the story in the car, Mom." Keith put one arm around Jimmy's shoulders and his other arm under his legs and carried him out the door.

Before I went to bed, I shook the last coins out of the bag and onto my quilt. There were twelve. I think Mom must have planned it that way. She should have bought the boys an extra present, though. Maybe she spoils me because she can't have me.

In the morning, I put on my cashmere sweater and looked this way and that way in the mirror. The dark chocolate color did match my eyes and turned my cheeks rosy.

"Don't make me a squishy sandwich for lunch," I told Dad when I walked into the kitchen. "And what are you putting in for dessert?"

"Change," he said. "We're out of cookies. You can buy ice cream."

"*Maybe* I will. I don't want to drip anything on this sweater."

"Pretty fancy to wear to school," he said.

"I know, but I can't wait for Susan to see it. She keeps a department store in her closet."

I left my jacket hanging open when I climbed on the bus. Susan saw the sweater as soon as she got on. She leaned over Marybelle, who had moved in beside me, and stroked the soft wool.

"Cashmere!" she said.

"It's neat, isn't it?" Marybelle said.

Susan ignored her.

"Sit down in the bus!" the driver yelled.

Susan took a seat in back and the driver shoved the bus into gear.

"Was yesterday your birthday?" Marybelle asked me.

"No, my mom made a trip to Reno. She brought me back the sweater and gave my brothers and me silver dollars to match our ages."

"Lucky you," Marybelle said, and that's all she said for the rest of the ride to school.

At lunch, Crystal turned her chair around to face me. Susan and Masaka came over to our desks. Susan made a big point of sitting with her back to Marybelle so she wouldn't dare join us.

Dad hadn't made my sandwich squishy. He'd made it too dry. I tried to push the peanut butter off the roof of my mouth with my tongue. When that didn't work, I pried it loose with my thumb.

Masaka made a face. "Gross, Gretchen!"

"Ya, gross, Grizzy," Spider said from his desk across the aisle. Arnold was eating with him and stuck his finger down his throat to make himself gag.

I laughed while I wiped my thumb on my napkin, but Susan knew I was embarrassed. She asked quickly, "What did your dad give you for dessert?"

"Change. I was going to get ice cream, but I forgot."

"I have two cookies." She pulled them out of her sack. "Here, take one."

I did.

Mrs. November doesn't bake, but she buys fancy things to eat. These weren't ordinary sugar cookies. They had chocolate zigzagging across them and a circle of raspberry jam in the middle.

Crystal watched me take my first bite. "I wish I'd forgotten my dessert."

It wouldn't have done her any good, because

Susan would have shared with me first.

Ms. Cooper was dismissing us when Mr. Swenson slipped in. She took a quick look around the room. There wasn't even a mess on the floor.

Mr. Swenson nodded approvingly as we filed out the door. Then he moved over to Ms. Cooper and placed his hand on her back. "Very nice," he said to her.

Ms. Cooper looked like she might faint from relief.

Susan didn't want to play tetherball. We just walked around the school grounds. "I feel crummy," she told me. "I hope I'm not getting the flu."

She looked even crummier the next day. She climbed on the school bus like an old lady and sank down in the first seat without even waving to me. After we got off, I caught up with her. She was still tottering along like an old lady. "What's the matter with you?" I asked her.

"I don't know. My head aches and I feel all sweaty."

"Why didn't you stay home?"

"I didn't want to be by myself," she said. "Mom had to drive Dad to work because his car is in the shop."

"Couldn't your sister stay with you?" I asked.

"No, Lindsi wouldn't do it. You know what a selfish pig she is." Susan put her hand up to rub her head and I saw that she had on blue earrings.

"Where did you get those great earrings? What kind of stones are they?"

"Turquoise." Susan didn't stop for me to see them closer. I guessed she felt too crummy.

About ten o'clock, when we were doing a reading test, Ms. Cooper noticed that Susan had her head down. "Susan," Ms. Cooper asked, "aren't you feeling well?"

"I'm sick," Susan mumbled.

Ms. Cooper felt Susan's forehead. "Is your mother home?"

"Maybe." Susan turned her head in my direction, and I could see her glazed eyes in her sweaty face.

She was really sick.

Ms. Cooper called the office for someone to get Susan. The secretary came. She helped Susan out of her seat and down the aisle.

The secretary had her almost to the door when Susan suddenly pulled away. "Just a minute," she muttered.

While we all watched, Susan staggered back to her seat, took off the blue earrings, and shoved them into her desk. Then she staggered back to the secretary, who helped her out the door.

CHAPTER 5

Rotten Bananas

❦ I called Susan's house when I got home from school.

"Susan is ill and can't come to the phone," her mother told me.

"Do you know what she has?" I asked.

"We won't know until the test results come back."

"Then she went to the doctor?"

"Certainly!" She might as well have said, "Who do you think gave her the tests, you little idiot?"

I said goodbye in a hurry and hung up.

I didn't have the nerve to bother Mrs. November the next day. But that evening, there was a story on the news about an employee of the Raindrop Grill coming down with hepatitis. The announcer said that anyone who ate at the restaurant between January 20 and February 18 should get an immune serum globulin injection immediately.

"Maybe that's what Susan caught," I said to Dad. "The Raindrop Grill is Mrs. November's favorite place. Poor Susan will have to get a shot."

"If she's already sick, it's too late for a shot," Dad said.

"She *is* already sick. What is hepatitis anyway? Can she die from it?"

"It's a liver infection. If someone has it and doesn't wash their hands, you can catch it from the food they handle. I think it's only fatal if you're run down when you get it. The last time I saw Susan, she looked like a healthy girl to me."

"She is, except for asthma," I said. "How long will she be sick?"

"Well, if it's really hepatitis, I don't think she'll be back to school for several weeks."

"Several weeks!" I bugged my eyes at him. "She's my best friend. Who will I play with this Saturday?"

"I can take you over to your brothers."

"No, thanks. Jimmy's the only good one, and he's too little."

The boys come to our house once a month, and I go over to Mom's house once a month. We used to exchange every other week. That suited Jimmy and Jason. Jimmy liked to be with Dad and Jason didn't seem to have anything else to do, but Keith and I wanted more time with our friends. I especially wanted to be with Susan.

I went to bed hoping she didn't have hepatitis. But she did.

Marybelle was the first one to tell me. When she got on the bus the next morning, she plopped down beside me. "It's too bad about Susan, isn't it," she said.

"She probably has the flu," I said. "She'll be back to school in a couple of days."

"No, she won't. She has hepatitis." Marybelle leaned forward to see how I took the news.

I pretended to see something interesting out the window.

At lunchtime, Crystal turned her chair around so we could eat together. Marybelle brought up her chair and plunked it beside our desks. She had another rotten banana and a smelly sandwich.

"Your lunch stinks," I told her.

"It's just tuna fish," Marybelle said.

Crystal wrinkled her nose. "Your mom probably bought a cheap brand on sale. My mom did that once. We had to throw out a whole casserole."

Marybelle took another bite of her sandwich. "It tastes okay to me. It's too bad about Susan getting hepatitis. She probably won't be back for a month."

"How'd you find that out?" Crystal asked.

"Everybody knows," Marybelle said.

I wished she'd swallow her food before she talked. I hated seeing the gummy bread and smelly tuna mixed up in her mouth.

After school, I called Mrs. November again. "I was wondering how Susan is," I explained.

"She's coming along as well as could be expected," Mrs. November said.

"Did you find out what she has?" I asked this as politely as I could.

"She has infectious hepatitis."

"Oh. Well, do you know when she'll be back to school?"

"No, I don't," Mrs. November said crisply. "We'll have to see how she does."

"Oh. Um, thanks. Tell her 'Good Luck' from me." I hung up the phone and sat on the couch wondering what I was going to do with my free days. Especially Saturdays when Dad played golf with his friends.

Crystal lived close, but she took ballet Saturday afternoons. Marybelle was the only other girl my age who was even in biking distance. I'd never been to her house and she'd never been to mine. I could invite her over, but I didn't like her very much after what she'd done to Susan's hair.

I guess she liked me, though. At lunch on Friday, she asked me if I wanted to come to her house the next day. I couldn't think of an excuse fast so I said, "Well, maybe I can."

She turned to Crystal. "You can come too if you want."

"I go to ballet on Saturdays," Crystal told her.

Marybelle turned back to me. "My house is that brown one, two houses from the corner. It's right across from the bus stop. Do you know which one I mean?"

I knew. Before Marybelle moved in, there had been a *For Rent* sign on the front lawn.

Dad left for his golf game at ten o'clock Saturday

morning. I finished the dishes and fooled around awhile. I didn't want to get to Marybelle's house before lunchtime. I was bored out of my mind, though. I got on my bike and rode down there.

Marybelle greeted me at the door with a big smile. "Come on in. Mom's making us lunch. We're having banana shakes."

Ugh. Rotten bananas. Just as I feared.

She took me into her kitchen and introduced me to her mom. Her mom has dyed black hair hanging in curls around her pasty face. The lines above her nose make her look like she's frowning even when her mouth is smiling.

"I'm so pleased to meet one of Marybelle's friends from her new school," she said.

"And I'm pleased to meet you, Mrs. Jackson," I said, eyeing the bananas left on the counter. Only brown spots. Not all black. Good.

Marybelle's mom and little brother, Corey, ate with us. Corey must have gotten his manners from Marybelle, because he talked with his mouth full of crackers and milkshake. He was into some long story about a horror movie he'd seen. He illustrated the monster by clawing the bare kitchen table with his fingernails.

Mrs. Jackson patted his hand. "Honey, somebody else wants to talk now."

He peered up into her face. "Who wants to?"

She ignored that and asked me, "Do your mother and father both work?"

"My mom's a computer programmer and my dad's the personnel director of the Zeot Corporation," I said. Then I figured I could be just as nosy as she was. "What does Marybelle's dad do?"

"Um, he's the produce manager of Safeway."

That explained the bananas.

"He manages all the Everett Safeways?" I asked.

"No, no. He manages just one."

Corey was still peering into his mom's face. "When did Dad get to be a manager?"

"Would you like more milkshake?" she asked me.

"No, thank you," I said. "I'm full."

Marybelle decided we should go into her backyard and swing.

"Me, too," Corey said.

Mrs. Jackson stroked his dirty little cheek. "Now let the girls play by themselves, honey. You know there are only two swings."

I followed Marybelle to her bedroom, where she went to get her jacket. When she opened the closet door, I saw there was only a shirt and saggy sweater on the hangers beside her jacket. I must have had a stupid look on my face, because she closed the door quickly.

"Mom's probably washing today," she said. "All my clothes are in the laundry."

All her clothes? It seemed to me she wore the same thing every day. "I live with my dad," I said. "I have to do my own laundry."

"You do?"

"It isn't hard. You just dump your stuff in the washing machine and then dump it in the dryer." My voice trailed off at the end of my explanation. It was dawning on me that I hadn't seen a washing machine in her house. All I saw were the plastic table and four plastic chairs in the kitchen. The kind you see stacked in front of hardware stores in the summer.

Out in Marybelle's backyard, two wooden swings hung from a big maple tree. We hadn't been on the swings five minutes before her brother appeared. He sat down on the porch step and planted his chin in his hand while he watched us.

He looked lonesome and little and ragged. Marybelle dragged her feet on the ground until she came to a stop. "Come on, Corey. I'll push you for a while."

She pushed him high into the air. I pumped until my feet touched the branches of the tree where his did. Marybelle pushed Corey harder, and he squealed with delight as he passed me to disappear into a mass of green leaves.

You'd think her arms would wear out. And I guess they did, because she let Corey slow down until she could catch the ropes holding his swing. "That's enough for me," she told him.

It was enough for me, too. "I think I better be going home," I said.

Marybelle reached out a hand to hold me back. "No, no. It's still early. We can play a game."

"We can play my spinning game," Corey said.

"Well, okay," I agreed. "For a little while."

We played Corey's game on the floor of their living room. It was frustrating for me, because my marker kept landing on "Go Back to Start."

Each time this happened, Corey crowed with glee. He and Marybelle didn't exactly cheat, but they carefully flicked the spinner so it would stop on the number they needed. I'd just caught on to this when the front door flew open and a small man with watery blue eyes stamped in.

Mrs. Jackson looked up from her magazine. "Why honey, you're home early. Are you sick?"

"I'm sick of taking a bellyful of crap," the man said. He stamped across the floor and into the kitchen.

"I'll warm you a cup of coffee," Mrs. Jackson called after him. She put down her magazine and heaved herself up from her chair.

I guessed the man was Marybelle's dad. I didn't ask, because Marybelle and Corey were exchanging worried glances.

We went on with the game, but I knew from their tilted heads that they were trying to hear the conversation in the kitchen. So was I.

Mrs. Jackson spoke so softly only mumbles came through the door. Every few minutes she'd shut up and there would be a burst from Mr. Jackson. "I know all about our bills," he shouted. "But I'm not sixteen and I'm not going to be treated like I'm sixteen."

More soft mumbles from Mrs. Jackson.

What had happened to Mr. Jackson, as near as I could tell, was he stacked fresh beets on top of old beets and got chewed out for it. By the real manager, I guessed. And this insulted Mr. Jackson, and he took off.

I wondered if this meant the end of his job. By the serious looks on their faces, I bet Corey and Marybelle wondered, too. They no longer carefully flicked the spinner, but spun it around any old way. The game dragged on until Marybelle's marker finally landed on "Home."

I stood up. "I guess I better be going."

She didn't try to stop me this time. She did walk me outside to my bike.

"Thanks for lunch and the game," I tried to tell her, but she was already running back to her house.

CHAPTER 6

Blue Earrings

❦ Marybelle ate at her own desk on Monday and Tuesday. This suited me fine, except for my curiosity. I itched to know the end of the story. Did her dad get fired?

In music class, she usually led the soprano section, but these days she was barely singing. I saw Mr. Monte look over his glasses at her three different times. If she kept on being quiet, he'd keep her after class to talk about her problems.

But she didn't. On Wednesday she was back to her old pushy self. Crystal and I went to Masaka's desk to eat. Marybelle butted right up to us and Masaka had to move to the corner to let Marybelle slide in her chair. It annoyed me.

I was so annoyed that I asked her right out, "How's your dad doing?"

"Fine," she said. "His headache's so much better that he went back to work today."

My hand holding my chicken sandwich hung in front of my open mouth. "What headache? Does Safeway think he had a *headache*?"

"Yes, my mom called them and explained that he had a migraine. Sometimes they're so bad we have to take him to the emergency room for a shot."

"I never heard of getting a shot for a headache," Crystal said.

"Migraines are a special kind of headache. They're very painful," Marybelle said.

Masaka nodded. "My grandma gets those if she eats chocolate. I've even seen her cry."

"Then why does she eat chocolate?" Crystal asked.

"She doesn't most of the time," Masaka said. "But she really loves it."

I shoved half of my sandwich in my mouth and sat chewing silently while they talked. Mr. Jackson hadn't said anything about a headache. He didn't act like he was sick, either. I bet Mrs. Jackson called up Safeway and told them lies so he wouldn't lose his job.

When I finished my sandwich, I stuffed the wrapping into my lunch sack. That was when Marybelle asked me over to her house on Saturday.

"I can't," I told her. "This is the weekend I spend with my mom. We'll probably go shopping for shoes."

"How neat for you," she said, but her slitted green eyes didn't look happy for me at all.

Mom, Jimmy, and I did go shopping for shoes. Keith

and Jason left us at the shoe store. They wanted to prowl the mall.

"They're going to spend all their dollars," Jimmy said. He was carefully looking over each running shoe displayed on the wall.

It didn't take me long to find the pair I wanted. It took Jimmy forever. I could tell he liked the purple ones best, because he fingered them the longest. But when he finally made a choice, it was a pair of black high-tops.

"Why are you getting black ones?" I asked him when we were seated in the chairs waiting for the salesman to bring our shoes.

"Because the kids in my class wear black ones."

"You should get what you like. Not what other kids like," I told him.

The salesman fitted me first. Jimmy watched me parade in front of the mirror. He pointed his finger at the All Star badge on the side of the shoes. "Susan has ones just like those."

"You got me," I said.

Keith and Jason met us in the middle of the mall. They were both carrying small packages. I elbowed Jason. "CD."

"Megadeth," he said back.

"Oh, Lord," Mom said.

"They're really good," Jason told her. "If you'd only listen to them, you'd see."

"You going to buy something?" Keith asked me.

I shook my head.

"Miser. You must have a million dollars by now." He turned to Mom. "Let's eat in the mall. I don't want to be late tonight."

"Teriyaki chicken. Teriyaki chicken. Teriyaki chicken," Jimmy chanted.

"Okay," Mom said. "Teriyaki chicken."

Keith hurried us through dinner.

"What's the big rush?" I wanted to know.

"Keith's got a date," Jason said.

"A date!" I couldn't believe it. "What's she like?"

Keith didn't say anything, so Mom answered me. "We don't know. We haven't met her yet. I'll meet her tonight."

"Mom's going to drive them to a movie," Jimmy said. "And her dad's going to pick them up."

"How convenient," I said. "Or inconvenient."

"Let's go," Keith said.

As soon as Mom hit the driveway, Keith had the car door open. Jason was right behind him. "I have to go to the john," he mumbled, stepping on my feet in his hurry to get out.

I limped to the door.

"Play a game of Monopoly?" Jimmy asked.

"All right," I agreed.

Jimmy got the game and I cleared the junk off the dining room table. He was sorting the slips of money when we heard a loud pounding on the bathroom door.

"Get out of there, Jason!" Keith yelled.

More pounding, then stamping into the living room. "Mom, tell Jason to get out of the bathroom. He's making me late on purpose. I have to take a shower, and he won't get out."

"Jason!" Mom hollered. "Let Keith come in the bathroom."

I guess Jason didn't, because the house shook with Keith's hammering.

"Let's go see," Jimmy said.

Mom beat us to the hallway. "Keith, stop that before you break the door."

"Well, you aren't making him get out of there," he said.

"Jason!" Mom really screamed this time.

Jason walked into the hall from the kitchen with an innocent look on his face. "You want me, Mom?"

"What's going on?" she asked him. "Weren't you in the bathroom?"

"I took a leak. It only took me a couple seconds."

Keith made a lunge for him. Jason leaped out of the way. Mom grabbed Keith. "Wait a minute," she said. "I thought you wanted to take a shower."

"I did until that snake locked the bathroom door and went out the window."

Jason pointed at his chest. "Me?"

Mom shook her head in disgust. "Jimmy, go get a nail so I can open this door."

Jimmy ran for the nail. Mom wiggled it in the hole below the doorknob until the latch popped open.

By the time Keith finished his shower and was ready to leave, Jason, Jimmy, and I were into the Monopoly game.

"Hey, you look all right," I said when Keith came into the dining room. "In fact, you look handsome." It was true. With his wild hair slicked down and his face scrubbed shiny, he looked better than I'd ever seen him.

Keith tried not to smile.

I was still thinking about my brothers when I went to school Monday morning. I told Crystal about Keith's first date.

"But what did your mom do to Jason?" Crystal asked.

"Nothing," I said. "She never does."

"My mom would have restricted me and my sisters for six months if we did anything like that." Crystal's shoulders quivered at the thought. Her family moved here from the South, and her parents are very strict with her and her sisters. They even have to say, "Yes, ma'am," to their mother and "Yes, sir," to their father.

Spider leaned across the aisle. "Turn your chair around, Crystal. The bell's about to ring, and I don't want to listen to Cooper yell again."

Actually, Ms. Cooper hadn't had to yell at us much lately. We all had gotten sick of it and were behaving ourselves. During "free time," I wrote Susan a letter about this.

Hi Susan,

How's your liver? I looked up hepatitis in the library. The book said your liver swells up and you turn yellow.

Ms. Cooper made us read about the spread of diseases in our health books. Like airborne ones and kissing ones. She made an especially big deal about washing hands. Too bad for you that guy at the Raindrop didn't wash his hands.

Ms. Cooper is calming down a little bit. The last time Mr. Swenson checked on us in the morning, we were all in our seats. He patted Ms. Cooper's shoulder and after he left, she read us a story.

Hurry up and get well. YES!

Miss ya,

Gretchen

Tuesday morning, Crystal didn't get on the bus. She didn't come to school, either. I hoped she hadn't caught hepatitis.

At lunchtime I planned to go over to Masaka's desk, but I'd barely gotten out my lunch sack when Marybelle dragged up her chair. At least she had grapes instead of a banana.

"Are you going to be home *this* Saturday?" she asked me.

"Maybe," I said. "It depends on if Susan's well or not."

Marybelle slowly picked the grapes off their stems. "You know, Gretchen," she said, "you wouldn't like

Susan so much if you knew what I know."

"What do you know?"

After she shot a wary glance Spider's way, Marybelle humped her chair even closer to my desk. "Mom and Corey and I were at the mall and we saw Susan and her mom in a jewelry store. I was going to go in and say hi to Susan . . ."

"Why would you say Hi?" I asked. "You know she doesn't like you."

"That's just it. I thought my mom could help me explain to Susan and her mom that the trimmer slipped and I didn't mean to shave her hair off."

"That's stupid," I said. "Susan knows it wasn't an accident."

"Well, I didn't mean to. And I was going to go in and try to make up, but my mom said to wait until they came out of the store and then we could invite them for a Coke. So we stood outside the jewelry store waiting for them. It was the one on the corner with the big glass windows."

Marybelle stopped to pop a grape in her mouth.

"Well," she continued, "Susan's mom was trying on earrings. She was getting them from one of those counter displays that swirl around. She put down the blue earrings she'd been trying on and moved to another display. Susan stayed behind. And then, guess what she did?"

I'd been sipping from my can of lemonade while I listened to Marybelle. I let the straw slide out of my mouth to ask, "So what did Susan do?"

"She took the blue earrings and put them in her pocket!"

I set the lemonade can down on my desk with a thump. "Susan did not!"

"Yes, she did. You can see real plain through those big windows. And I saw her put the blue earrings into the pocket of her jeans."

I stared into Marybelle's green eyes to see if I could tell if she was lying. She just stared back and gave me one of her shrugs.

"What day was this?" I asked her.

"The Saturday before Susan got sick."

That was the Saturday my brothers stayed at my house. Susan could have gone to the mall with her mother, but her sister would have gone with them.

"Where was Lindsi?" I asked.

"I don't know. I don't know any Lindsi. I only saw Susan and her mom. You don't have to believe me if you don't want to."

I was trying not to believe her, but the picture of Susan staggering to her desk to shove the blue earrings inside kept flashing in my head.

CHAPTER 7

Head-on Crash

🍎 Susan called me Saturday morning.

"You're finally out of bed!" I said. "Are you well now?"

"I feel okay," she answered. "But the doctor wants me to stay in the house to get my strength back."

I imagined her wobbling around her peach-and-yellow bedroom. "Just what's the matter with your strength?"

"Who knows?" she said. "But they won't let me go to school until I see the doctor next week."

I let out a sigh. "So I'll probably have to go to Marybelle's house today."

Dead silence on the line.

I wondered if this meant Susan had seen Marybelle watching outside the jewelers and was afraid she would tell me, or if Susan thought I was a traitor for playing with Marybelle while she was sick.

"I was over at Marybelle's two weeks ago and saw her closet," I added quickly. "All that was in it was a shirt and a raggedy sweater and her jacket. She made some excuse about her clothes being washed."

"The closet was almost empty?" Susan asked.

"Right. Except some junk on the floor with the old blue sweatpants that she wears sometimes."

"They must be poor," Susan decided. "I'd like some sweatpants, though. Mom always buys me stuff she thinks will impress her customers."

"I wish I had all the stuff you do."

"Try getting it torn and then see what your mom says."

"My mom would never notice."

Susan giggled. "But your mom's fun."

"True," I said. "You come back to school right after the doctor's appointment, okay? Or I'll be sick from smelling Marybelle's rotten bananas."

"I'll try," Susan said.

After we hung up, the phone rang again. It was Marybelle.

"I was thinking," she told me, "that you could come down here on your bike today and have lunch. And then we could ride up to your house. You could steer half the way and I could steer half the way. Unless you're going over to Susan's."

"No, she has to get her strength back. She'll probably be at school sometime next week."

"Well, do you want to come over then?"

"I guess so. But not for lunch," I said.

"You don't *have* to eat here."

"I know. I know I don't. But there's some pizza left in

our fridge. I'll see you in a couple of hours." I hung up feeling dumb for agreeing to go over there and dumber for insulting her food.

When I got to Marybelle's house, she and her little brother had cartoons on the TV. I sat down to watch the show with them.

"It's lucky you didn't come for lunch," Marybelle told me during the commercial. "Mom's got a permanent going on in the kitchen."

I thought she meant her mom was giving herself a perm until Corey piped up. "I hope she gets a big tip."

Corey's mind was still on the tip when Mrs. Jackson opened the kitchen door. "Did she give you a big tip?" he asked.

Mrs. Jackson put one hand to her lips and, with the other hand, pointed to the kitchen. "Shh."

Corey clamped his lips shut.

"Are you girls about ready to leave?" Mrs. Jackson wanted to know.

"Just about," Marybelle said.

"I'm going to be busy another hour. Why don't you take Corey with you?"

I tried to imagine three of us on one bike. Nooo.

Marybelle bit her fingernails between sneaking glances at my face.

Corey whined, "Marybelle! I want to go!"

"You girls run along," Mrs. Jackson said. "Corey can bring his color crayons in the kitchen."

"No!" Corey yelled. "It's stinky in there."

"Listen." Marybelle took hold of his arms so he would listen. "As soon as I get back, I'll play the spinning game with you. Three times."

"Promise?" He asked tearfully.

"Promise!"

She grabbed her jacket, and we split.

It was nine blocks to my house. I steered for the first five blocks.

The sun had come out, so I tied my rain poncho around my waist before we changed places. "Remember to stay on the side of the road, and there's a stop sign two blocks up," I said.

"I know. I know. I've ridden a bike before." She walked the bike down a driveway and then jumped on the pedals.

For someone who'd ridden a bike, she was pretty wobbly. I perched nervously on the seat and peered around her shoulder.

"The stop sign's ahead," I warned her.

"I can see it," she said. She was going more smoothly now.

She slowed down at the stop sign, looked to the left and to the right, and then sped up.

"Wait, wait," I hollered. "There's a truck!"

A big oil truck was bearing down on us from the left. I dragged my feet to stop the bike. Marybelle shot a glance at the truck and pumped harder.

"Wait!" I screamed.

Too late. I heard the screech of the truck's brakes, felt the thump as it hit the bike's back wheel, and then the searing pain as I slid across the pavement.

CHAPTER 8

Roll Me Over

❦ Big hands touched me gently on my back. "Are you all right?" the oil man asked me.

"My arm," I mumbled.

I rolled over and lifted my arm. Shreds of my shirt hung from the red, raw sore that went from my wrist to my elbow.

"We'll get that tended to. Where do you live?" The oil man had kind brown eyes.

"I want my dad," I told him.

"We'll get you to your dad. Where do you live?"

Two old ladies hovered behind the oil man. "That bicycle didn't even stop for the stop sign. I saw the whole thing," one old lady said.

My arm stung. My arm stung awfully bad.

Marybelle stepped in front of the old ladies. "She lives two blocks up the street. In the whitewashed brick house."

The oil man scooped me up. He opened the door of

his truck and placed me inside. I saw Marybelle wheel my bike to the curb as the oil man climbed in the cab and started his motor.

He explained and explained to my dad that he couldn't stop his truck in time to avoid hitting me. Dad said he understood. He said it was lucky I only had a scrape.

I looked down at my bloody arm. A scrape?

After the oil man left, Dad told me, "Come on. We'll go to the clinic and get you cleaned up."

"I don't want a shot," I said.

"We'll see," Dad said.

I saw. I got a shot. I also got the arm cleaned up with burning medicine. "That should take care of it," the nurse said. "You'll feel better now."

I felt like I was going to puke all over her white shoes.

When we got home, my bike was leaning against our porch. "That was nice of your friend to bring it back," Dad said.

"She isn't my friend. And I don't think she's nice. Something bad happens whenever she's around." I leaned down to inspect my bike. "The back fender's bent and the spokes are smashed."

"I can straighten them out," Dad said.

"What about the chipped paint?" I asked. "You'll have a hard time matching that."

"I'll manage," he said.

Sunday morning, Marybelle and her mom knocked

on our door. Dad invited them in. "We just came by to see how Gretchen is," Mrs. Jackson explained.

"She's a bit bruised, but she'll be fine," Dad said.

Bruised? He thought I was *bruised*?

"If you hadn't dragged your feet, we would have been clear of the truck." Marybelle said this in a quiet voice. But she said it.

This made me really, really mad. Before I could say that if she'd come to a full stop at the stop sign, she would have seen the truck, her mom spoke up.

"It doesn't matter, Marybelle. You were driving." She turned to my dad. "I want to give you this to help pay for Gretchen's shirt."

Mrs. Jackson took a ten-dollar bill from her purse and held it out to Dad.

He took it!

I was so embarrassed, I could hardly say good-bye to them. I kept looking at my feet until Dad closed our front door.

"You shouldn't have taken her money," I told Dad. "I think they're poor. Mrs. Jackson gives permanents in her kitchen. You probably got the money she earned yesterday."

He didn't offer to give it back.

That's the one thing not so good about my dad. He's not a generous person. Not like Mom. She'd change her last dime into nickels and give you one.

And Dad didn't even buy me the shirt. Mom did.

I picked up the TV remote so I didn't have to think about these things. Nothing was on, of course, but basketball.

Early Monday morning, I hacked the sleeves off an old sweatshirt. "You're going to wear that to school?" Dad asked me at breakfast.

"I don't like anything covering my sore. When something rubs on it, it hurts." I threw my jacket over my shoulders and went off to school.

Spider leaned across the aisle to eyeball my arm. "Whoa! Who pounded you?"

"An oil truck," I said.

"An oil truck! You blind or something?"

"No, Marybelle is. She was steering my bike and I was riding on the seat."

"Ah," he said, "Jackson strikes again."

All this attention from Spider put me in a very good mood. I stayed that way until lunchtime when Arnold bumped my arm dragging his chair up to Spider's desk.

"Ye-ow!" I shrieked.

"Take it easy on her," Spider told him. "She tangled with an oil truck."

I poked Crystal. "Let's go eat with Masaka so I don't have to put up with Marybelle."

Much good that move did me. We'd barely opened our lunches when she plunked down beside us.

"Did you buy a new shirt?" she asked me.

"No," I said, just as coldly as I could.

That didn't faze Marybelle. "Aren't you going to?"

"You want a new shirt?" Masaka asked.

"Not particularly," I said.

"Well, my mom gave you the money," Marybelle said.

Crystal wrinkled her forehead. She wears glasses, but she still wrinkles up her face. Maybe her glasses need to be even thicker. "Why did your mom give Gretchen money for a shirt?" she asked Marybelle.

"Well." Marybelle stopped to put her half-eaten apple on Masaka's desk. "You see, Gretchen and I were riding to her house on her bike . . ."

I knew what was next. This time I got my say in. "Marybelle was steering and she didn't stop for a stop sign so she didn't see the oil truck coming at us."

"I saw him! We had plenty of time to get across the street. You dragged your feet so I couldn't pump."

"You mean I dragged my feet so we wouldn't get clobbered." I turned to Masaka and Crystal. "You should see my bike."

Masaka shuddered. "I don't want to. Your arm's bad enough."

Marybelle went back to eating her apple with a mad look on her face. If she'd tried to explain any more, I was going to say her mom didn't pay for my shot at the clinic. But she kept her mouth shut.

Just before music on Tuesday, there was a knock on our classroom door. Ms. Cooper gave us a warning look before she moved to answer the knock. It was

Mrs. November. And right behind her was Susan! I felt my face break out in a grin from ear to ear.

"We just came from the doctor," Mrs. November told Ms. Cooper, "and he said Susan was fine. She couldn't wait until tomorrow. I hope it won't interrupt your class to have her come in now."

"Oh, no, no, no, no," Ms. Cooper said. "We've missed her, too. And we're delighted to have her back."

Right! I was hopping up and down in my seat like Robbie does. Mrs. November saw me and wiggled her fingers in a greeting before she gave Susan a kiss and disappeared.

Susan walked to her desk with that secret look on her face. It comes on whenever she knows people are watching her. I hissed, "Ssssu-ssan."

She slid a grin my way.

We walked together to the music room. We didn't dare talk, though, because Ms. Cooper was keeping a beady eye on us. She'd spotted Mr. Swenson standing in front of the faculty room with the nurse. When Ms. Cooper reached them, Mr. Swenson put his hand on her shoulder and guided her inside.

Mr. Monte made a big fuss over Susan. As soon as he saw her, he sang out, "Hello Susan!" to the tune of "Hello Dolly." We all laughed.

"I've got some grand news for seven of you," he announced. "I wanted it for all of you, but Mr. Herbert said both rooms of sixth graders couldn't squash into the faculty room." Mr. Monte's gray eyes twinkled behind his glasses. He knew he was confusing us. I think he makes his announcements like mystery stories so we'll listen in death-bed quiet.

"It's Mr. Herbert's sixth graders' big show," he went on, "so I had to give in to their teacher. And they're bringing the food. Or making the food, I hope. I'm not sure hope is the right word."

Robbie let out a guffaw.

"This luncheon Mr. Herbert's students are giving for the faculty is on April tenth. If any of the chosen seven can't come that day, let me know well in advance."

Arnold raised his hand. "What are seven of us supposed to be doing?"

"Why, singing, of course. You're the entertainment. I've been thinking that 'Oh, What a Beautiful Morning' would be a great song for you. What do you think?"

No one knew what to think.

"Ms. Cooper and I will confer on choosing the seven singers, because they will have to be out of class for rehearsals."

Out of class! Great. Especially since I was one of the best singers. Not as good as Masaka. Or Spider. Spider sang all the time. I should know. I sat next to him. He even hummed while he did his math.

"Any questions?" Mr. Monte asked.

Marybelle raised her hand. Mr. Monte nodded her way, and she asked him, "When will we know who's chosen?"

"Oh, I imagine I can tell you the names next Wednesday."

I hardly heard his answer. It had hit me that Marybelle was a good singer too. Susan croaked like a frog and didn't have a chance.

She and Crystal ate lunch with me. Marybelle butted in our conversation after dumping an apple core in the garbage. "Did you find your blue earrings, Susan?"

Susan's eyes, I noticed, seemed to dart three ways at once. "Yes," she mumbled, "they were still in my desk."

Marybelle gave me a knowing smirk before going back to her seat.

"Your mom buy you the earrings?" I asked.

"No, Grandma gave them to Lindsi. I just borrowed them."

What? Lindsi didn't lend her things. She's her mother's clone. You can't touch anything she has.

I sat munching on my sandwich, wondering. Who was lying? Marybelle or Susan?

CHAPTER 9

The Spy

❦ Wednesday morning we had an earthquake drill. By the time Mr. Swenson rang the all-clear bell and complimented the school on responding quickly, we had missed our music period.

"Wait a minute! Wait a minute!" Robbie called out when Ms. Cooper told us to take out our math books.

"Robbie, please raise your hand before you speak," Ms. Cooper said.

"But we *have* to go to music today," Robbie insisted. "Mr. Monte is going to tell us who the entertainers are."

"Oh." Ms. Cooper reached over to her desk. "I have the list here. I'll read the names to you."

A shiver ran over me as I listened carefully for my name.

Ms. Cooper read, "Masaka Tada, Harlan Black . . ."

I knew they'd get it, but what about me?

"Arnold Smith . . ."

I hadn't even thought about him.

"Eric Jorgensen, Gretchen Griswald . . ."

I melted into my seat, limp with relief.

"Katie Oswald and Robbie Blanchard." Ms. Cooper put the list back on her desk and moved toward the board.

Marybelle waved her hand in the air.

Ms. Cooper was busy writing 1.53 ÷ .16 on the board.

"Ms. Cooper, I have a question," Marybelle said.

Ms. Cooper turned around. "Yes?"

"I was . . . I was wondering how you chose the singers."

"Well," Ms. Cooper said, "we chose them for their singing ability and their good behavior."

"Yes, but." Marybelle wrung her hands nervously. "Yes, but Robbie doesn't have good behavior."

Robbie stood up, indignant. "I'm good in music."

"You're always talking out," Marybelle told him.

"Not when I'm singing. I'm good when I'm singing."

He is. I love it when Robbie sings. His voice reminds me of a flute. Sweet and high. Most of the time his face is twitchy, but when he sings, it turns soft and he looks like an angel.

"I'm sure Robbie will add to the group," Ms. Cooper told Marybelle. And that was that.

Mr. Swenson came in our room just as we were finishing our lunch. Ms. Cooper jumped to her feet when she saw him.

"Students," she ordered, "please clean up around your desks, put your refuse in the garbage can, and get ready for recess."

Except for her flushed face, she was acting like a real teacher. Mr. Swenson patted her shoulder as we marched out of the room.

Crystal, Masaka, Susan, and I decided not to join a game. Instead, we paraded around the baseball field. Spider was on the mound. "Come on, Grizzy," he yelled. "I'll put you out in three pitches."

"In your dreams, Harlan," I yelled back.

"He looks so cute," Crystal said, "with his hair flopping over his eyes."

I thought so too, but I wouldn't have said it.

When we passed the swings, Marybelle hopped off and began walking beside me as if she belonged in our group. "I know why Ms. Cooper picked Robbie instead of me."

"Because he has a better voice?" I suggested.

"No, she doesn't like me because of what I saw her do."

I wasn't going to give her the satisfaction of asking what she saw. Susan marched silently on the other side of me. But curiosity got the better of Crystal. "What did you see?"

Marybelle took in a big breath. "Well, you know how Mr. Swenson can't keep his hands off Ms. Cooper . . ."

Masaka turned to frown at Marybelle. "What are you talking about?"

73

"About Mr. Swenson and Ms. Cooper. What do you think? He still had his hands on her after we left the classroom."

"How do you know?" Masaka asked.

"Because I turned around and looked. And Ms. Cooper saw. And she saw me the other time, too."

None of us asked her about "the other time," which Marybelle was obviously expecting us to do.

She should have known better than to gossip in front of Masaka. Masaka never says anything mean, and she challenges anybody who does. I've seen Masaka's mother. She has a flat, calm face. I can't imagine her ever gossiping. But I bet Mrs. Jackson's customers get an earful.

The bell rang, ending our recess. "I'll beat you all to the door," Masaka said. And off we flew, leaving Marybelle behind.

I guess Marybelle doesn't give up easily, though. Thursday, Susan and Crystal ate lunch with me. I didn't think Marybelle would have the nerve to join us. It was obvious Susan never intended to speak to her again.

But at recess, Susan stayed inside to pass out colored paper for our art lesson. Marybelle caught Crystal and me going out to the playground. "Ms. Cooper just put on fresh lipstick, didn't she?" Marybelle asked us.

I shot her a funny look. Who cared?

This didn't stop Marybelle one bit. "I hope Mr. Swenson doesn't come for a visit and not see Susan's in the room. She'll get the surprise I got. Susan's mom would make a really big stink about that."

I admit I was curious. But I kept my mouth shut and waited for Crystal to egg her on. "What surprise did you get?" Crystal asked.

"Well." Marybelle's green eyes glittered as she moved in between Crystal and me and took hold of our hands.

I don't really enjoy holding hands with people. Especially with someone like Marybelle. My mom's the only one who gives me kisses and hugs. Maybe I've lived too long with my dad to get used to people touching me.

"You see," Marybelle said, happily waving our hands back and forth, "one day last week I left my spelling book at school. . . ."

Her voice sounded as if she were telling a fairy story to her little brother. "What day?" I asked.

"Oh, I don't know. Before we had the test. So it must have been last Thursday, I guess. Or Tuesday. I don't remember. But I know my mom drove me back to school to pick up the book."

"Doesn't your dad take the car to work?" I'd never seen a car in front of her house, except when her dad was home.

Marybelle nodded. "He usually does. But Mom had to get new curlers for her perms, so she drove him to Safeway. Anyway! Mom took me to school and I ran in. . . ."

I was about to ask if the janitor didn't lock the doors when Marybelle explained that, too.

"It was lucky for me all the teachers hadn't left, and the main entrance was still open. I ran down the hall to our room. Our door was shut tight, and the blind was pulled over the little window like Ms. Cooper pulls it when we see films. We hadn't seen a film that day, so I thought the covered window was strange. I opened the door softly and peeked in."

Marybelle stopped walking and looked first into Crystal's face and then into mine. "Guess what I saw?"

"What?" Crystal and I said together.

"Mr. Swenson kissing Ms. Cooper!"

"No way," I said. "Mr. Swenson's a grandpa. He brought his grandchildren to our winter concert."

Marybelle shook her head. "That doesn't matter. Old men are always getting pretty woman. Don't you ever watch the soaps? And Ms. Cooper is a dumb teacher, and she has to keep her job some way."

Crystal wasn't interested in our argument. She was interested in the kiss. "What exactly were they doing?"

"Well." Marybelle started walking again, swinging our hands. "Mr. Swenson's back was to me. They were over by the windows, and he had his head bent over hers and they were really going at it."

"Did they see you?" Crystal asked.

"Ms. Cooper did. That's the whole point. She must have heard the door and she opened her eyes, stared right at me, and started pushing Mr. Swenson away."

"Did she say anything?" Crystal wanted to know.

"No. I backed out fast. I didn't want her mad at me, so I wasn't going to tell anybody. But then she went and chose Robbie instead of me. So I don't care."

"Robbie's a good singer," I said.

"Yes, but he's always bad. And I'm a better singer than Katie. Even you have to admit that, Gretchen."

I didn't admit anything.

After we were back in our room, I hardly paid attention to making my collage. While I snipped pieces of colored paper, I sneaked glances at Ms. Cooper. She was walking around the room helping kids with their designs.

She is kind of pretty. She has her hair cut short with bangs and this makes her eyes look large. But I didn't know how old she was.

"How old do you think Ms. Cooper is?" I asked my dad when he got home from work.

"Oh, I don't know," he said. "Twenty-two, twenty-three, I guess."

"How old do you think Mr. Swenson is?" I asked Dad at dinner.

"Beats me," he said, helping himself to huge spoonfuls of mashed potatoes.

He and I pig out on mashed potatoes. Mom's big on raw vegetable salads, and her figure looks it. She told Dad he'd better watch his diet, because he was getting flabby around the middle. He didn't like her saying that one bit.

"Mr. Swenson's a grandpa," I said, "so how old does that make him?"

"Anywhere from forty-five to seventy."

"You aren't any help," I told him.

Dad raised his eyebrows. "What's all this preoccupation with age?"

"Marybelle said that she saw Mr. Swenson kissing Ms. Cooper."

"What? When was your friend Marybelle supposed to have seen this?" Dad'd stopped fooling around and was looking very serious.

I wished I'd never mentioned the kiss.

"Marybelle isn't exactly my friend," I said. "I don't even think I like her. She said she went back to school one afternoon to pick up her spelling book, and she saw them in the classroom kissing. She said they'd pulled down the blind on the door window."

"And left the door unlocked?" Dad asked.

"I guess."

"Did anybody else see this?"

"No."

"Hmmm," Dad murmured.

"Marybelle said Mr. Swenson can't keep his hands off Ms. Cooper." I added that to back up the story. I didn't want to sound like I believed any old thing.

"Have you seen Mr. Swenson with his hands on her?"

"Well, he does pat her sometimes," I said.

"Where?" Dad asked.

"On her shoulder."

"When?" Dad asked.

"When she gets nervous about how we're behaving while he's in the room."

Dad shook his head slowly. "Poor grandpas have to learn not to pat young women in these times. They even got our former governor for that."

"What governor?" I asked.

"Our governor. The governor of Washington State. Aren't you learning anything in school?"

"You don't have to get mad," I told him. "I wasn't the one who said I saw them."

"But were you entertained when your friend was telling you this gossip?"

"Well," I said, "it was about my teacher."

"And do this girl's parents tell stories, too?"

"The mother lies. Her father just whines."

Dad nodded. "I think you can find ways to get attention other than spreading gossip. That kind of story can be painful for your teacher and the principal and his wife."

"Telling my own dad is spreading gossip? Okay, I won't tell you anything anymore." I jumped out of my chair, dumped my plate in the sink, and didn't even ask about dessert.

The next morning my mind was stinging from being accused of gossiping. I didn't feel like talking to anyone at recess, so I played in the outfield on Spider's team. I missed a fly ball and that made me even crabbier.

Marybelle came prancing up when I was walking back

to the school building after the bell rang. "I wonder if Mr. Swenson will hang around our room today," she said.

"Who cares," I snarled. "My dad thinks you and your mother make up stories."

The smile dropped off Marybelle's face. "You and your dad can think anything you want, Gretchen Griswald. I know what I saw."

She yanked open the school door and let it slam behind her.

CHAPTER 10

Fat and Lazy

❦ Thursday night, Mom called. She said the boys weren't coming for the whole weekend, because Keith wanted to be with his girlfriend. She said they'd just come for Friday evening and Sunday afternoon. And Keith was bringing his girl on Friday.

"He's bringing his girl?" I said to Dad. "I wonder what she looks like. What kind of girl can Keith get?"

"I imagine he'll have the standard model with legs and arms," Dad said.

With legs and arms, maybe, but what about a brain or a face? I wondered all the next day about that.

I was at the living room window as soon as I heard Mom's car drive up. Keith's girl was a small, curly-haired blonde. I couldn't believe it.

My three brothers ushered her in together. "This is Angela," Jimmy announced.

She gave Dad and me a shy smile while she moved closer to Keith. He dropped a protective arm around her shoulders.

"I'll get Angela a drink," Jimmy said. "What have you got?"

"Grape juice or root beer," I said.

"What do you want?" Jimmy asked Angela.

"Grape juice would be fine," she said.

"You can sit down on the couch," he told her and hurried off to the kitchen.

Keith sat on one side of her and Jason on the other. Dad sat in the leather chair and I sat on the footstool in front of him.

Nobody said anything.

Angela stared at her pink fingernail polish. I twirled a strand of hair around my finger, feeling like the ugly sister.

Total silence.

Suddenly, I heard myself burst out, "I always wanted curly hair."

"Oh, mine isn't naturally curly," Angela said. "It's straight as a string. And thin. I have to have a perm to make it fluffy."

"It's cute," I said.

She squinted her eyes at me. "You could do yours. Have it cut short and permed all over your head. It would look cuter than mine, because your hair's thicker."

I decided I liked Angela. And if I hadn't made Marybelle mad, her mother could give me a perm.

Jimmy came into the room carrying a tray with six glasses filled with grape juice. Dad started up from his chair. "Do you want some help?"

"No," Jimmy said. "I can handle it."

He stood in front of Angela first. She took one of the glasses. "There's a napkin for you, too," he said.

Angela reached for a napkin and placed it in her lap. Jimmy went on to Keith and Jason and then over to me and Dad.

After Jimmy put the empty tray on the coffee table, he perched on the arm of the couch to drink his grape juice. I could feel Dad squirm nervously behind me. We have a beige rug in the living room and grape juice would make a mess on it.

It wasn't Jimmy that spilled his juice, though. It was Keith. He was shifting his glass from one hand to the other so he could put his arm around Angela. He looked down at her as he did, letting his glass tip to the side.

"Keith, watch it!" Dad called out.

Too late. A blob of juice landed on Keith's jeans. He jumped up, spilling the rest of the glass onto the floor.

"Gretchen, get a towel!" Dad ordered.

I ran into the kitchen for a towel. When I came back, Keith was on his knees trying to sop up the juice with his paper napkin.

"Here, I'll do it." Jimmy grabbed the towel from me and scrubbed it over the rug.

Keith sat back on his bottom. "I'm just a big lunk."

"And fat and lazy," Jason added.

I thought Keith would hammer him for saying that. Instead, he turned his face away from Angela to hide the blush spreading over his nose and cheeks.

"The grape stain isn't going to come out, Dad," Jimmy said.

"You might as well let it go for now," Dad told him. "I'll have the carpet cleaners come in tomorrow."

"I'll pay for it," Keith offered.

"That's all right," Dad said. "The rug needs cleaning anyway."

This surprised me. I expected Dad to at least make him mow our lawn.

Keith pulled himself to his feet, gathered up our glasses, and carried the tray and towel into the kitchen. Jimmy bounced into Keith's place on the couch.

"What would you like for dinner?" he asked Angela. "We could send out for pizza. Or do you like teriyaki chicken?"

"I guess so," Angela said. "I don't really remember ever having it."

"If you'd had it, you'd remember," Jimmy assured her. "It's real good. Dad, why don't you call up Yamamoto's and order teriyaki chicken?"

I turned around to see what Dad was going to say.

"All right," he said.

Amazing.

After everyone left and I was in bed that night, I imagined tilting a head of brown curls this way and that and Spider knocking himself out to please me.

The next morning, the carpet cleaners came. They

dragged in a vacuum and a plastic wand attached to a hose. The cleaner with a saggy face stared at the grape juice stain. "It's going to take some strong stuff to get that out."

"Do the best you can," Dad said.

He opened the door so the chemical stink would flow outside. It didn't seem to do much flowing. I stayed in the garden, planting sweet peas, until the cleaners lugged out their tools and drove away in their truck.

After dinner, we closed the front door and sat down to watch a video. In the middle of the film, sharp pains speared my chest. "That smell is hurting my lungs," I told Dad.

"It's bothering me, too," he said. "We'd better get out of the living room."

He rewound the video, put it back in the box, and went to the wall to turn the thermostat up high. "Don't you want to turn that down and open the door?" I asked him.

"No," he said, "we have to heat the room to pull the chemicals out of the rug. Cold air won't do it."

"Pulling the chemicals out will kill us," I said.

He shook his head. "I doubt it. In the morning, we'll open the doors and windows to get rid of them."

"I'm glad my bedroom's in the back." I took my social studies book in there and read until I was sleepy.

Dad was the first one up and the one who opened the doors and windows on Sunday morning. By the time I got up, a hard cough was barking up from his chest. "Do you think you're getting a cold?" I asked.

"No, it's just from inhaling fumes."

"Why don't you go to the Chec Medical Center? They probably could stick a needle in you. Or pump out your stomach," I added evilly.

"It's my lungs, not my stomach. As soon as the fresh air gets through the house, I'll be fine."

Dad and I shivered through breakfast. I was coughing by the time we finished. To get away from the chemicals, I went into my bedroom to study.

The social studies chapter Ms. Cooper had assigned was icky. I hate to read about masses of soldiers massacring pitiful bands of Indians. By the time I heard Mom's car arrive, I had a list of generals and chiefs and dates of battles. Ms. Cooper is big on facts. This is good, because then I don't have to think too much about crying Indian babies.

I closed my book and went into the living room.

"How come it's freezing in here?" Jimmy was asking.

"What *is* that smell?" Mom wanted to know.

"I had the rug cleaned yesterday," Dad said. "The chemicals haven't quite dispersed."

"They certainly haven't." Mom took a sharp look at me. I was trying to swallow a cough that had sprung from my chest.

She turned back to Dad. "This is no place for

Gretchen to be. I'll take all the kids to my house until this place is thoroughly aired."

Dad nodded. He couldn't say anything because he was covering a torrent of coughs with his hands. Mom watched him with a disgust that shot old fears through me. I'd seen that expression on her face when I was little and one of their quarrels was coming on.

"You just have to have everything immaculate, don't you?" she said. "Even if your compulsiveness kills you."

He didn't answer her this time, either. He was bent over, gasping for air.

Mom's face softened. "Gretchen, pack some clothes for both you and your dad."

I didn't move off my chair, because Dad was shaking his head.

"Right now," she told me. "Before we're all poisoned."

I hurried to get some underclothes and pajamas. When I returned to the living room, Keith had already taken Jimmy and Jason outside. While Dad clutched his chest, Mom pushed him out the door.

I got in the backseat of the car with the boys. Even after Mom shoved Dad into the front seat, he kept protesting, "I'm fine. I'm fine now." He followed this with another coughing fit.

Mom started up the motor. "You sound fine. But if you think I'm letting my daughter back in that house before the chemicals are out, you are also certifiable."

I turned to Keith with a questioning look.

"She means your dad can be certified to be placed in a nut house," he said.

"How'd you suddenly get so smart?" I was serious when I asked him this. I'd always thought of Keith as a big, dumb bully.

Mom tilted her head towards the backseat to answer my question. "Age, college prep courses, Angela, and good genes."

I believed the Angela part. Since Keith'd been going with her, he'd turned a lot nicer. I didn't know about the genes, though. Except for Mom's. Mom was smart. Maybe I'd never expected much of Keith because I knew his dad was a drunk. A certifiable one.

Mom made a detour to the market on the way to her house. She bought six big Dungeness crabs. Cracked crab is my very favorite food.

Dad likes it too, but he said he wasn't hungry and he thought he'd just stretch out on the couch for a bit. He was asleep in ten minutes. The rest of us helped Mom get dinner on the dining room table. She tied towels around each of our necks.

"This feels like a baby's bib," Jimmy said.

He happily cracked his crab shells, though, squirting juice on Jason and me. "Hey, watch it," Jason said.

Jimmy just grinned. I think he liked having all of us together. "You could stay here all the time," he told me.

I pulled the thick meat from a crab leg and popped it into my mouth. "But what about Dad? He'd be all alone."

Jimmy looked over at Mom. "Dad could stay too. Couldn't he?"

"Your Dad and I aren't married anymore," she said. "You know that."

Jimmy heaved a sigh. "I know."

"*I'm* never going to get a divorce," Jason announced.

"What makes you think you're ever going to get a girl?" Keith asked.

He was obviously proud of having Angela. He talked to her on the phone for an hour after dinner.

Dad was awake by then, and he thought he should go on home.

"No," Mom told him, "give the chemicals more time to clear out. You can sleep in Jimmy's room and Jimmy can sleep with Jason."

I usually slept in Jimmy's room when I visited, but Mom said this time I could sleep with her. Before we fell asleep that night, she whispered in my ear, "I wish you could stay here all the time, too."

I know she was trying to say how much she loved me, but it made me sorry for my little self and Jimmy. When I was Jimmy's age, I'd wished and wished she'd come back home and we'd be a family again. That was never going to happen. Bad luck for Jimmy and me.

CHAPTER 11

Nasty Smile

❦ I heard the bedroom door open and then Keith say, "Hey, Mom, aren't you going to work today?"

"What time is it?" Mom's voice was foggy with sleep.

I turned over in the bed to stare at Keith. "How's Dad?"

"He's fine. He took off in a taxi a half hour ago. And it's ten to eight."

"What about Jimmy?" Mom asked.

"I already fed him. He and Jason are out waiting for their busses. I gotta go." Keith disappeared from the doorway.

"I must have forgotten to set the alarm," Mom said.

I threw off the covers. "I'll be late for school."

"No, wait." Mom was smiling one of her wicked smiles. "Let's me skip work and you skip school. We'll go shopping and buy you something fancy. Then we'll have a luscious lunch."

"Dad would never play hookey from his job," I said.

Mom heaved a sigh like Jimmy does. "I know. Your dad is a man who doesn't like change."

I wore my tennis shoes to the mall, but carried them in a bag when we went into the Garden Restaurant. Mom caught me peeking under the table at my new, fancy shoes.

"They do look pretty on your feet," she said.

We had a great time except for the tiny uneasiness about music in the corners of my mind. There wasn't a music *period* on Mondays, but Mr. Monte could call a rehearsal for the entertainers.

Mom dropped me at my house about five o'clock. I immediately called Susan to ask her if there'd been a rehearsal. Her mother answered the phone. "May I talk to Susan?" I asked. I'm always polite to Mrs. November.

The line was silent so long I thought maybe she'd left to get Susan, but she hadn't. "You've been ill?" Mrs. November asked.

"Not really. My dad and I got coughs from the chemicals in the rug."

"Chemicals in the rug?" She made it sound like I was making this up.

I hurried to explain. "The rug cleaners came to clean our rug and they must have used strong chemicals that hurt our lungs."

"Oh." Another silence. "Well, you can talk to Susan for a minute."

A minute?

"Hello," Susan said.

"What's the matter with your mom?" I wanted to know.

"Why?" she asked.

"Because your mom said I could talk to you for 'a minute.' Are you in trouble?"

"No."

"Listen, did Mr. Monte call a rehearsal for the entertainers today?"

"No," she said again. And that's all she said.

"Don't you want to hear why I didn't go to school?" I asked.

"Of course." It didn't sound like "of course." It sounded like "If you must tell me."

I launched into my whole story anyway. I got to the part where Keith woke Mom and me up, when Susan interrupted. "Just a sec."

I could hear Mrs. November's voice, but I couldn't tell what she was saying. Susan must have had her hand over the speaker.

I waited and waited. Finally Susan came back on the line. "I gotta go," she said.

"Why? Don't you want to hear what we did?"

"You're coming to school tomorrow, aren't you?"

"Yes," I said.

"Tell me tomorrow then."

I hung up the receiver, slumped down on the couch, and tried to figure out why Susan cut me off.

Maybe, maybe Susan did steal those earrings and her mom found out and put her on restriction. Maybe she didn't want to tell me that over the phone. Maybe she was too ashamed to talk about it.

She would tell me eventually, I was sure. We always told each other everything.

On the bus the next morning, Crystal and Marybelle were sitting together, whispering, which registered strange in my head. But then Crystal likes gossip and Marybelle is good at that.

I took a seat next to Masaka. She asked me if I'd had the flu.

"No, my Dad and I got coughs from the chemicals the carpet cleaners used on our rugs."

Masaka's eyebrows flew up. "You were poisoned? Are you all right?"

"Sure." I saw Susan had gotten on the bus. I could hardly wait to tell her about my new cream-colored shoes with the little heels and the lace-up tops.

But Susan didn't even look back to where I was sitting. She took a seat by the driver. I caught up with her after we got off the bus.

"What's your big hurry?" I asked. "Are you in trouble?"

"No, no. I wanted to check my social studies book. Ms. Cooper put off the test until today."

I followed Susan into our classroom and then to her seat. I was barely launched into my story when Crystal came over to join us. I noticed she sat on the desk across from us instead of on Susan's desk with me.

I had barely finished telling about my new shoes when Crystal waved her hand in my face. "Oh, my sister has a pair like those."

I was going to ask where she got them, but Crystal had jumped off the desk and was heading for her seat. And Susan was pulling out her social studies book. If she was worried about the test, why hadn't she taken her book home?

Obviously, though, she didn't have anything more to say to me. There was nothing to do but go to my seat. Just before I sat down, I glanced back at Marybelle. A nasty smile curved around her little white teeth.

CHAPTER 12

The Reject

🍎 I didn't do very well on the social studies test. I was remembering when Susan and Spider sat together in second grade. They squirted each other through milk straws. Susan got caught. Her lips trembled under the stern scolding the teacher gave her, but she didn't cry.

At recess, we'd huddled behind the backstop. She cried then. I told her the teacher would never remember to phone her mom, because of all the bad things Robbie would do in the afternoon. This turned out to be true. Robbie hopped out of his seat so many times the teacher went crazy and yanked him down to the office.

"You have five minutes to finish the quiz," Ms. Cooper announced.

Panicking, I scribbled down as many answers as I could. But what was the name of the big battle Crazy Horse fought? What was the name?

"Time's up!" Ms. Cooper said and collected our papers.

It was just one lousy test, I told myself. At recess, I'd walk with Susan behind the backstop and get her to tell me what was bugging her. That didn't happen.

Crystal and Susan went over to Masaka's desk to eat lunch. I expected to join them after I bought some ice cream. But when I got back in the room with my ice cream, I saw Crystal carrying Katie's chair to Masaka's desk. Katie was following with her lunch sack. There was no room left for me.

Susan stayed in at recess to help Ms. Cooper again. I walked out to the baseball field all by myself. Kids were crowded around Jim and Spider, who were choosing sides. Spider spotted me and tossed me the extra mitt. "We need a shortstop and you're it."

Eric jumped up and down in front of Spider. "What about me? What about me? I can play shortstop."

"You can play in the field." Spider walked out to the mound. Arnold crouched behind the plate.

"Batter up!" Spider yelled.

Robbie stepped up with the bat. He missed Spider's fastballs twice, popped a foul behind Arnold, and then hit a grounder right to me. I zoomed it to Jean on first base. She stumbled trying to catch it. The ball hit Robbie on the leg and he flopped on the ground, yowling with pain.

I didn't even care.

Because of the test, we hadn't had music in the morning. But after recess, Ms. Cooper excused the seven singers for our first rehearsal.

"Robbie, what happened to you?" Mr. Monte asked as we filed into the music room. "You're limping."

I didn't think Robbie's limp was bad, but Mr. Monte never misses any detail about us.

"I got hit by a ball," Robbie said. "It'll go away in a few minutes."

"I hope so," Mr. Monte said. "I'm planning a solo for you in 'The Tennessee Waltz.' Ms. Cooper is from Tennessee and the waltz is a lovely, romantic song. I thought we'd sing that for her."

Mr. Monte played the song on the piano and then had us sing along with him. All the time I was thinking, romantic? Ms. Cooper? Did Mr. Monte know about her and the principal?

I imagined Ms. Cooper being kissed by Mr. Swenson. Would his false teeth slip? Would they make his S's whistle when he whispered to her? Every time he said he was proud of the ssstudents in Lawsson SSSchool, the first graders had to smother their giggles in their fingers so their teacher wouldn't send them out of the gym.

Mr. Herbert was another thing. His sixth-grade girls giggled over him. But that was because of his wavy black hair and soft black mustache.

Mr. Monte was taller than Mr. Herbert and he had a mustache, too. But it was short and bristly and, except for blond hairs hanging over his ears, his head was bald. We loved him anyway, but not romantically.

Mr. Monte lifted his hands from the keys. "Gretchen, let's have a little more volume, please."

When we had the song down to Mr. Monte's satisfaction, he moved Robbie to the front and had him sing the first verse a cappella. His clear, high voice filled the room with such a sweetness, shame overcame me. I had never said I was sorry my ball hit him.

After school, Susan ran to the bus and sat behind the driver. I raised my eyebrows at her as I passed by. She kept looking out the window. It went on that way all week.

I tried to tell Dad about it.

"Can't you call Susan on the phone and talk this over?" he asked.

"I've tried that. Mrs. November says Susan's busy."

"Maybe the problem is at home," Dad suggested.

"I've thought of that, too. But we've always shared our problems. Even the home ones."

"Maybe 'always' is in the past," Dad said. "You're becoming young ladies."

"I don't feel like a lady. I feel like I smell or snitch or do something kids hate."

This brought a worried frown to Dad's face. "Some kids play with you, don't they?"

"Sure. Spider and Masaka. And the kids in the singing group. But Crystal doesn't talk to me, either. I don't care so much about her. I care a whole lot about Susan. It's making me sick."

"Tell you what," Dad said. "I'll drive you over to Susan's Saturday morning on the way to the golf course. I'll walk up to the door with you and tell Mrs. November you've come to visit Susan and I'll be picking you up in an hour."

"You can't even play nine holes in an hour."

"Well, as a favor to me we'll go back to the course and you can wait in the clubhouse until I finish eighteen holes."

I held out my hand. "It's a deal."

Saturday morning, Mrs. November listened to Dad's speech and then let me come in. What else could she do?

Susan was in her room painting her toenails. She looked surprised to see me.

"I can only stay an hour," I said quickly.

"Oh. You want to paint your nails, too?"

"No, that's okay. I'll just watch." I sat on her bed trying to think how to start my questions.

Susan finished her right foot and put lumps of cotton between the toes on her left foot. Her sister Lindsi pushed open the bedroom door. "Have you seen my denim shorts?"

"No," Susan said.

Lindsi narrowed her eyes. "Are you sure you didn't 'borrow' them like some of your *friends* do?"

That crack went right by me.

"Your shorts are probably in the hamper," Susan said.

It was then I noticed Lindsi was wearing the blue earrings.

"Great earrings," I said to her.

She flicked one with her finger. "I think so. Grandma gave them to *me*. Something Susan has trouble remembering."

"I only wore them once," Susan said. "It didn't kill you."

"Once!" Lindsi jerked her head toward the bed. "You had them for a month while I went wild trying to find them."

"That's because I was sick. I couldn't get them out of my school desk when I was sick."

"You had no business putting them in there. And the least you could have done was tell me where they were. *And* you'd better not know where my shorts are!" Lindsi flounced out the door.

"I told you they're in the hamper," Susan yelled.

"Sisters!" she said to me. "You're lucky you only have brothers."

I was too stunned to say that brothers weren't perfect. Over and over in my head went the words, *Marybelle lied, Marybelle lied*. Susan hadn't stolen the blue earrings.

"I have to go to the bathroom," I said.

"You come right back," Susan said.

"Of course. What else?"

While I washed my hands in the bathroom sink, the bandage on my ripped hangnail got soaked. I looked in the medicine cabinet to see if there was a box of Band-Aids. There was. I taped a small one around my thumb, closed the cabinet, and opened the bathroom door.

Mrs. November stood in the hall facing me. "What were you doing in there?"

"I was going to the bathroom."

"You were doing more than that." She marched into the bathroom and opened the medicine cabinet.

"I also took a bandage because mine got wet when I washed my hands." I pulled the tape away from my reddened hangnail. "See."

She glanced briefly at my thumb before she went back to moving every bottle and tube to see if anything else was missing. Finally she closed the cabinet. "Gretchen, you go directly into Susan's room and stay there until your Dad picks you up."

I walked stiffly into Susan's room and planted myself in front of her. I could feel my face burn hot. "Susan," I said, "tell me what's going on."

She concentrated on pulling the cotton from between her toes.

"Come on," I insisted. "Your mother treats me like a criminal and you hardly speak to me."

"Well, my mom thinks I should expand my circle of friends."

"You have plenty of friends," I said.

Susan kept her face down, tossing the cotton pieces

one by one into her wastebasket. "Mom thinks we don't need to be together so much."

"So much? Or does that mean we aren't ever going to be together?"

"Well, sure. We'll be together in games at school sometimes."

"Sometimes," I repeated and turned to her door. "I think I'll wait for my dad on your front steps."

She didn't try to stop me from leaving.

CHAPTER 13

Wild Animals

❦ "I guess things didn't go too well," Dad said when I climbed into his car.

"That's an understatement." I huddled down in the passenger seat to stare out the window at nothing.

He didn't grill me on the way to the golf course. And before he left for his game, he gave me food money in case I got hungry while I was waiting for him.

His clubhouse isn't a fancy place like the ones you see on TV. If you want to eat, you have to drop quarters in the machines that are lined up in a cement hallway. I chose orange pop and potato chips. I meant to get plain salted chips, but I pushed the wrong button and got barbecued ones instead. They tasted like cardboard doused in fake smoke and chili powder.

I walked outside to feed them to the pigeons that hang around the lawn. A white-haired man came hobbling up the path. "Young lady," he said in his squeaky old voice, "don't you know that junk food isn't good for those poor creatures?"

"Pardon me. I didn't know you were the keeper of the birds." I stalked off before he could tell me what a mouthy young thing I was.

It was two hours before I saw Dad dragging his golf cart along with some buddy of his. I called out from under the tree where I was sitting. He waved good-bye to his friend and came over to me. "Ready for dinner? How about stopping at the Red Robin on the way home?"

When I didn't answer, he added, "You eat too many cookies out of the machines?"

"No," I said.

"Well, do you want to go to the Red Robin?"

I almost snarled, "No!" But I was starving.

Dad waited until we were on our fudge sundaes before he asked, "Won't you tell me what went on at Susan's?"

I didn't want to discuss being humiliated, but he'd asked so nicely, I blurted out the whole miserable story.

At the finish, he thoughtfully stirred the remaining ice cream in his bowl. "Maybe you should have asked Mrs. November before you took a Band-Aid out of her cabinet."

"You don't know Mrs. November. She doesn't like to be interrupted with little things like that."

"Maybe you could have asked Susan, then."

I slapped my spoon onto the placemat. "Susan and I have been in each other's houses since we were six years old. You think she'd ask me if she could have a little

Band-Aid? And anyway, that's not the point. You don't understand any of it!"

Dad silently paid the check, silently drove us home, and said nothing when I didn't kiss him goodnight. He did open my door before he went to bed. I was under my covers, staring at the ceiling with my lamp still on.

"Gretchen," he said softly, "parents would always like to keep their children safe and happy. Unfortunately, it isn't possible. I hope you find a new friend soon."

"Who?"

"I don't know who. But your brothers will be here next weekend."

"Very exciting," I said.

"Maybe not, but they're company. Sleep tight, honey." He closed the door. And it was just in time. Tears had started pouring down my face. My dad never calls me honey unless I'm sick. I wished I were sick so a doctor could give me something to make the hurt go away.

The hurt didn't go away. I fell asleep to a dream that hurt even more.

I was in Mom's kitchen making dinner by myself. I'd decided on a scalloped potato casserole. I don't know why scalloped potatoes. I've only seen my grandma make them once.

I put the sliced potatoes, onions, ham, and milk in a large roaster pan so there would be enough food for all my brothers. But things shifted like they do in dreams.

On the kitchen table were baked sliced potatoes in an oval bowl, the kind you use for a vegetable dish of green beans or carrots.

Mom sailed in while I was poking the potatoes with a fork. She was about my age. "The potatoes are still hard," I told her.

She waved a hand like it was nothing. "Put them in the microwave for five minutes and they'll get soft."

"But this won't be enough for dinner," I whined. "What should I do?"

"Go ask Keith," she said and sailed out the door.

I found Keith in his bedroom playing a game on his computer. A boy I didn't know was with him. When the boy saw me, his nose wrinkled as if he were looking at mouse droppings.

I moved closer to put a hand on Keith's shoulder, but Keith was concentrating on his game and didn't notice.

The boy snarled at me, "What are you doing here?"

I backed away from the light of the computer and cowered in the dark corner of the room. Marybelle had told the boy something terrible about me.

When I jerked awake from the dream, it was still night-time. Fear of Marybelle's lies hovered over me. What was I going to do?

What was I even going to do during school lunches? I could beat Katie to Masaka's desk. But if Susan and

Crystal were there, maybe they wouldn't want me. Face it, I told myself in the dark. They don't want you.

Could I pick another girl? Maybe Amy, who was a bookworm and read while she ate? I really didn't know how to butt into her reading. Just take my chair and plop it down beside her like Marybelle did?

I couldn't do that.

I couldn't sit by myself, either, with my face swelling bigger and bigger like a red balloon. Even Spider would wonder why nobody sat with me.

I thought of asking Dad to let me live with Mom so I could go to a different school. He might if I insisted. He'd be so hurt, though. It was too mean to do to him.

You have to stop being a baby, I told myself. You'll just have to get a library book and go up to Amy and ask if you can read with her.

But what if she looked up and said, "Well, I guess it's okay." I'd feel like an idiot.

I really wanted to be a baby. I wanted to cry and have someone comfort me. I did cry a little bit before I fell asleep again.

In the morning light, I pulled myself out of bed, telling myself, You're going to have the guts to do it. You'll just have to have the guts to try it.

During library time on Monday, I noticed Amy was reading a book about cats. I found the section on wild animals and chose *A Field Guide to Animal Tracks*. It had mountain lions, jaguars, and lynxes in it.

I could feel my face flush when Ms. Cooper said, "Time for lunch," and Crystal made a beeline for Masaka's desk. I didn't look back to see who else joined them. I took my book and chair and lunch sack and hauled them across the room to the aisle where Amy sat.

"Mind if I sit down and read with you?" I asked.

Amy looked up from her book, surprised. "Oh, sure. That'd be fine."

She moved her carton of milk to give me room to put my lunch on her desk. "What are you reading?" she asked as I settled into my chair.

I handed her the field guide. She flipped through the pages. "Oh, it's got bobcats in it. My mom lived in Montana when she was a kid. Her dad was a ranger. And she tried to make friends with a bobcat.

"Bobcats hunt mostly at night, and she left food in her backyard for him. She gradually moved the food toward her porch. When her dad caught her doing this, he explained to her that when a wild animal hunted, it didn't think. It operated purely on instinct. He told her if she wore her new bunny slippers near the bobcat it might smell rabbit and that would trigger the wild animal circuit in its brain and it wouldn't remember that my mom was a friend."

"Scary," I said.

"True," Amy agreed. "My mom hasn't changed much, though. Last summer she made friends with a blue jay. She lined peanuts along our deck and through the sliding glass door. The blue jay hopped inside and perched on a chair. Only the blue jay wasn't house-broken, and we all laughed at my mom when she had to scrub the chair seat."

"Does she still have it for a pet?" I asked.

"Sure, but she doesn't coax it inside anymore. On Halloween, after we scooped out our pumpkins, Mom put the pulp in a pan on the deck. Her blue jay pecked out all the pumpkin seeds."

"I'd like to have a blue jay." I said. "They're pretty."

Amy smiled. "They are."

Then she settled down to eating and reading her book, and I settled down to mine.

"Let's clean up before recess," Ms. Cooper called out.

I closed my book and stuffed the plastic sandwich wrapping in my lunch sack. Trying to sound as casual as possible, I asked Amy, "How about eating with you tomorrow?"

"Sure. I've got a book on birds at home. I'll bring it for you."

On the way to my desk, I saw Crystal had stopped to talk to Marybelle. They shot sneaky glances at me. I pretended I didn't notice and went right out to the baseball field after Ms. Cooper dismissed us.

"You're on my team," Spider said.

That was okay with me.

We had singing practice after recess. Masaka walked to Mr. Monte's room with me. "Amy's nice," she said.

"I think so. And smart. She wasn't easy to know when she first came to our school this year because she reads all the time. She's such a bookworm, you know." I rattled this out in an embarrassed rush, because Masaka was probably wondering why I was eating with Amy. She wouldn't ask me right out. It isn't a thing Masaka would do.

"Thursday is the tenth," Mr. Monte told us when we were seated. "Just two more days until you sing at the luncheon. So this afternoon, I want you all to sound like birdies."

Mr. Monte can get away with saying things like that.

"And," he went on, "I want you to feel joyous when you sing 'Oh, What a Beautiful Morning.' Come on now. Joy! Joy! Joy!"

He lifted his baton, and we raised our joyous voices. It wasn't until the hour was over that misery crawled back into my stomach.

The next few days, Crystal ignored me, except when she was whispering to Marybelle. Susan's mouth pinched into a tight "O" when she had to pass me in an aisle. Once she tried to turn it into a small smile. I couldn't smile back.

Amy brought me the bird book and a book about the migration of butterflies. I brought her one of Jimmy's funny books, *The True Story of the Three Little Pigs by A. Wolf.*

She laughed so hard over the story that the egg in her

egg salad sandwich flew out of her mouth. "I'm sorry," she said, wiping up the dribbles.

"No problem," I said. "The book's *hilarious*." That was one of Amy's words. If I kept eating with her, I was going to sound like a bookworm, too.

Thursday morning, I put on my best blouse and my newest jeans, wove my hair into a French braid, and fastened the braid to my head with a sparkling gold bow.

"Wow," Dad said when I appeared in the kitchen. "You're going to knock the other class dead."

I wouldn't mind knocking their teacher dead.

Mr. Herbert was there when Mr. Monte marched the seven of us into the faculty room. Ms. Cooper was at the head of the table with a vase of red roses in front of her. Mr. Herbert sat on one side of her and Mr. Swenson sat on the other. The rest of the school staff were seated around them. Except for the librarian. She'd taken the students into the gym to see a film while their teachers ate.

Mr. Herbert's kids put plates of spaghetti at each place on the long table, set a big bowl of salad in the middle, and a basket of rolls wrapped in a napkin beside a dish of butter patties. Mr. Herbert had evidently taught them how to give a luncheon.

After the rolls and salad had been passed and the kids were seated and eating, Mr. Monte raised his baton. Joyously we sang "Oh, What a Beautiful Morning." Everyone at the table clapped.

Mr. Monte whispered to Robbie. Robbie crossed the room to stand beside Ms. Cooper and sing the first verse of the "Tennessee Waltz." Tears sprang into Ms. Cooper's eyes. One of her hands was on the table and Mr. Herbert reached over and covered it with his hand. Mr. Swenson looked down at them fondly.

We joined Robbie in the chorus. When we finished this time, everyone clapped even louder. We made our bows as Mr. Monte had taught us to do.

Mr. Swenson pushed his chair back to stand. "Thank you very much for your songs. And they were very appropriate ones, too. We will miss Ms. Cooper next year, but we all wish her and Mr. Herbert a long, happy life together."

He gave Ms. Cooper a fatherly pat on the back and it was then I noticed the sparking diamond on her finger. I was still staring at it when Mr. Monte gave me a gentle tap to remind me to march out of the faculty room with the other singers.

CHAPTER 14

Liar, Liar

On the way to the bus after school, I ran up to Marybelle and grabbed her by the back of the neck. "You're a liar," I told her. "You're a stinking liar. You lied about Susan. She never stole those earrings from a jewelry store."

Marybelle wrenched herself free. "So, big deal. I saw somebody who looked like her."

"Oh, no you didn't, you stinking liar. And you didn't see the principal kiss our teacher either."

A couple of boys stopped to watch us. She gave them a quick sideways glance and started easing toward our bus.

Before she could get away, I grabbed her neck again. I hated her so much I wanted to choke her dead. "What did you tell Susan and Crystal about me? And don't bother lying some more. I know you did, because otherwise we'd still be friends."

"What makes you think everyone always wants to be

your friend?" She gave me a hard poke in the chest to make me drop my hand, and then she climbed on the bus.

Half the kids were staring out the windows. I got on the bus, too, ignoring everybody, even Susan, and found a seat by a sixth grader who was busy undoing the rings of a puzzle. All the way home, I steamed.

I knew that stinking Marybelle told lies about me. She knew she did. But she was never going to tell me anything. And even if I knew what she said, how would I convince Susan and her mother it was a lie? What if the lie spread all around the room and Amy believed it? What could I do then?

Dad wasn't going to be any help with this. This was a time a girl needed a mother. I called her after dinner. I started the whole conversation out wrong, because I asked her, "Did anybody ever tell lies about you?"

Mom laughed. "Not that I know of, love. I'm afraid any tales people told about me were probably true."

"Well, a girl told one about me and made me lose my best friend."

"That's too bad. Can't you straighten things out by telling your friend the truth?"

"If she'd believe me," I said. "And if I knew what the lie was. The girl who tells them makes up such good stories, I even believed some of them myself."

"Ah. There are those clever liars in this world. They're

usually bitter, inadequate people trying to get even with the ones they're jealous of. The best thing to do is stay clear of them."

"Yes, well, thanks for the advice," I said, even though she hadn't been any help.

"Your brothers are coming over Saturday," she reminded me.

"The whole weekend?" I asked.

"Saturday and Sunday. Angela's going to Portland for her grandmother's birthday."

"I'll tell Dad. Good-bye, Mom."

"Good-bye, sweetie," she said. "I love you."

All night long, I tried to think of ways to choke the truth out of Marybelle. And a way to make Susan stand still and listen. I couldn't even think of one possibility.

The next morning, I dragged myself to school. The kids were buzzing about Ms. Cooper's engagement to Mr. Herbert. "Did you know about that?" Amy asked me at the coat hooks.

"I found out when we sang for them yesterday. I guess that was the luncheon celebration. She had red roses in front of her plate, and he held her hand."

"I wish I could have been there," Amy said.

"That's the bell," Ms. Cooper called out. "You're all supposed to be in your seats." She was standing in the front of the room, holding a cage with a hamster in it.

Spider leaned over to me. "That's her wedding present."

"It is? Who gave it to her?"

Spider shook his head. "You are so gullible."

Gullible?

"The fourth graders have gone on a field trip today," Ms. Cooper said. "They have asked us to take care of their hamster, Furry Black. His cage needs to be cleaned. And he needs to be fed and have his water changed at noon. Who would like to do this during lunchtime?"

"Does he bite?" Eric asked.

"He has never bitten one of the fourth graders, but I think he should be handled gently."

"I'll take him!" Robbie yelled.

"Not until you learn to raise your hand before you talk," Ms. Cooper said.

Ten kids raised their hands, including Marybelle, who waved hers wildly in the air.

"All right, Marybelle. We'll let you be the one," Ms. Cooper decided.

Robbie groaned, and Marybelle looked like she'd swallowed one of the parakeets that were printed on her bright white T-shirt.

She pranced up to the counter by the sink as soon as Ms. Cooper asked us to clear our desks for lunch. She took the hamster out of the cage, petted it, and cooed to it. "Furry Blacky. Furry Blacky."

I watched her with rage boiling in my stomach.

"Does Marybelle like animals?" Amy asked me.

"Weasels, probably," I said.

Marybelle held the hamster up to her face and rubbed her cheek on its fur. "Pretty Furry Blacky." She knew the whole class was watching her.

"Its name is Furry Black, not Blacky," Robbie said.

She smirked at Robbie, then let out a sudden shriek. The hamster dropped to the ground like a rock.

Ms. Cooper put down her coffee cup and rushed to Marybelle. "Did he bite you? Where? Show me."

"No, he didn't bite me." Marybelle pulled out the front of her wet T-shirt. "Look! He peed on me."

I burst out laughing.

Amy was shocked. "Gretchen! Her T-shirt looks brand new."

Ms. Cooper frowned at me and the rest of the kids who were giggling. "Dropping a hamster isn't funny. It could be hurt."

"I've got it! I've got it!" Robbie called out from under the desks. He stood up, holding the hamster. "He's all right. He scampers real fast."

"Oh, good." Ms. Cooper sighed with relief. I don't think she was up for any more disasters in our class.

"I'd better take care of him, though." Robbie tucked the hamster safely in his pocket, moved to the sink, and took the water bottle off the side of the cage.

He gave Marybelle a shove away from the faucet. "You can clean your shirt in the Girls' Room."

"That's a good idea. You go help her, Crystal," Ms. Cooper said.

As Crystal and Marybelle went out the door, I must have looked pleased, because Amy was still watching my face.

"It's a long story," I said to her. "You don't know Marybelle. She tells lies about people. Awful lies. But she tells them so well, you believe them."

"Did she tell lies about you?"

"Yes. And she said Susan shoplifted when she didn't. She said she saw the principal kissing Ms. Cooper when Ms. Cooper was engaged to Mr. Herbert. At least that lie got shot down. I haven't figured out what she told about me."

Amy sucked her orange thoughtfully. When she'd dropped the empty orange skin onto her napkin, she looked directly into my eyes. "Is that why you eat with me instead of your old friends?"

"Yes, because I can't make Marybelle tell me what she said. It must be something really bad, because nobody will tell me. Not even Susan." My voice choked on the word "Susan" and I ducked my head to hide my eyes.

"If you find out the lie and straighten it out with your old friends," Amy said softly, "you won't have to eat with me anymore."

Oh, no, I wanted to say, I wouldn't do that. I wouldn't stop being her friend like Susan had stopped being mine. I knew Susan always did what her mother made her do, but it hurt.

I didn't know how to explain all this to Amy and I was

afraid I might cry again if I tried, so I said, "Don't be silly. You have the best books. And you can say something besides 'neat' or 'cool.' By the way, what does *gullible* mean?"

"It means you'll believe anything," Amy said.

CHAPTER 15

Brother Keith

Saturday afternoon, Dad took the boys and me to a movie. The movie was supposed to be funny, but it didn't make me laugh. On the way home Jimmy said, "You look so sad, Gretchen. Don't you want us to be here?"

I put my arm around his narrow shoulders. "Sure I do. I just have a little problem I can't solve."

For dinner, Dad picked up teriyaki chicken for Jimmy and ice cream bars for Jason.

Keith did away with four pieces of chicken and a mound of fried rice before he leaned back in his chair to lick his ice cream bar. "Okay, now, Gretchen, let's get your little problem solved."

"Wow, big man," I said.

"He thinks he is," Jason said, "just because he won the wrestling title at school."

"I'm impressed," I told Keith. "I didn't even know you were competing. I thought you just knocked Jason around."

"Well, Mom can't do everything. I still have to keep

Jason in line. But on to your little problem. Start at the beginning. The first thing that happened was . . . ."

"The first thing that happened was Marybelle Jackson moved into our neighborhood. It turned out that she was a liar. A very good liar. She told lies about Susan November, she told lies about our teacher, and now she's told lies about me."

Keith held up his hand. "Whoa. Let's take this one lie at a time. Real slow, so we get all the details. Exactly what, where, and when did she tell a lie about Susan November. November, huh? Does she have a sister Lindsi?"

"Yes," I said. "And she's part of the lie. Or how I found out it was a lie."

"All right now. From the beginning."

"He's taking journalism, too," Jason put in.

"Keep your trap shut, Jason," Keith ordered. "Now, Gretchen. . . ."

I looked around the table. Dad seemed interested. And Jimmy was leaning forward in his chair. So I began my story, right from the beginning, putting in all the details, right down to Mrs. November inspecting the medicine cabinet.

When I finished, Keith sat quietly stroking his chin. "Hmmm. Hmmm."

"It's impossible," I said. "That liar Marybelle lost me my best friend."

"No, no, no," Keith corrected me. "It isn't impossible. We just have to plan this carefully. We have to get all the parties together and face Marybelle with her lies."

Jason's eyes brightened. "You mean like we did with our real dad? When everyone got together and told him he was a drunk?"

Hope drained out of me. "You dummies. That isn't going to work with Marybelle. I've already tried that. I faced her with the lie about seeing Susan at the jewelers and she just lied some more by saying she must have seen someone who looked like Susan."

Keith shook his finger at me. "Yes, but you said Marybelle told both you and Crystal about your teacher. Marybelle's going to be trapped there. Now, you drag out some of that loot you hoard and give a pizza party. Invite all the girls to the party and leave the rest to brother Keith."

"Keith, no way is Susan coming over here. Mrs. November won't even let me talk to her on the phone."

"That's easy," he said. "You don't have to talk to her. I'll call up Lindsi and invite both her and her sister."

"You don't know Mrs. November," I said.

"No, but I know Lindsi, and Lindsi finds ways to do what Lindsi wants to do."

"I've got to see this," I said.

"Right now." Keith tossed his empty ice cream stick onto his plate.

I started to get up to follow him to the phone, but he brought the phone to the table. "What's the number?"

I told him, and he dialed it. "May I speak to Lindsi, please? This is Keith Richards."

Keith enjoys saying his full name. Once, for a joke, Mom bought him a silver ring with a skull and crossbones on it. It looks just like the one the Rolling Stones' guitar player wears. Keith loves that ring.

"Hi, Lindsi girl," Keith said into the phone. "I'm having a little pizza get-together tomorrow and wondered if you'd like to come over."

I waited.

Keith was grinning. "What time's your mom have to be at the open house?"

And still grinning. "See you at two o'clock then. And drag along your little sister."

Frowning. "Hey, she's just my half sister. Does that count me out?"

Half sister. That was me Lindsi was putting down.

"Ri-ight! See you both tomorrow." He clicked off the phone and handed it to me.

"The rest is up to you, Gretchen. Get Crystal and Marybelle over here at two o'clock and we're in business. You better have a cake and pizza delivered at three-thirty. Hmmm." He was thinking again. "Is there extra ice cream in the freezer? We ought to serve root beer floats to start this thing off."

"There's a gallon in the freezer," Dad said. I was a bit surprised he was going along with all this. It was more Mom's sort of thing.

I called Crystal first, told her about the pizza party, and said that Susan and her sister were coming, maybe she should, too. I could feel Crystal hesitating and then deciding if Susan was coming maybe she should, too.

Sweat broke out on my forehead when I dialed Marybelle's number. She answered. I blurted out in one breath, "This is Gretchen. A bunch of girls are coming to my house tomorrow at two o'clock for pizza. Do you want to come? Susan and Crystal are coming."

Keith was shaking his head. "Real smooth."

I placed my hand tightly over the speaker. "I hate her guts."

There was a long, long pause. Marybelle was doing more than thinking this over. Did she smell a trap?

"I guess I shouldn't come if it's just girls," Marybelle finally said. "Corey gets lonesome when he has no one to play with."

"It's okay to bring Corey. My little brother Jimmy's here. He'll be glad to have someone to play with, too."

Another long pause. "I'll see if we can get a ride."

Before I could say Jason and Keith would bike them over, I heard the phone clunk down. She came back on a few minutes later. "It's all right. We'll come at two o'clock."

"Oh. Oh, fine," I managed to say.

"But I don't know how long we can stay."

"That's all right. We'll be glad to have you." I clicked off the phone and wiped my sweaty face with a napkin.

"And the scene is set!" Keith announced.

CHAPTER 16

The Lying Game

🐞 At exactly two o'clock there was a knock on our front door. Keith answered it. "Lindsi girl! Come on in."

Susan followed behind her. She gave me a polite nod while Lindsi was giving Keith her dazzling smile.

"Where's everyone?" Lindsi asked, taking in the empty living room.

"Dad and my brothers are in the family room. You don't want to go in there. That's where we dump our sleeping bags when we stay here on weekends."

"But where's Angela?"

"She's in Portland," Keith said.

Lindsi raised her perfectly plucked eyebrows. "Interesting."

Keith placed his hand on her back and started to guide her to the kitchen. "How about you and me making root beer floats?"

She twirled away from him. "You go ahead. I'll be there in a second."

As soon as Keith was through the kitchen door, Lindsi took a hard hold on my arm. "Mom and Dad are showing off one of the houses she decorated. She doesn't know we're here. So keep quiet about it."

"Sure," I said.

She let go of me and headed into the kitchen. I wanted to rub the place where she'd pinched my arm, but Susan was standing in the middle of the room looking miserable. I answered the doorbell instead.

It was Crystal. "Hi," she said to me. And then gave a louder, happier, "Hi," to Susan.

I prayed Keith knew what he was doing, or I was going to be one stupid monkey by the end of this day.

Marybelle was next with her little brother hopping beside her. "Happy birthday!" he said to me.

"Oh, it isn't my birthday, Corey," I told him. "It's just a get-together."

"That's good," he said, "because we don't have any presents. Where's your brother?"

"He's around. Jimmy!" I hollered.

Jimmy appeared from the hallway. "This is Corey," I said. "And Corey, this is my brother, Jimmy."

"Come in the family room," Jimmy told Corey. "I'll show you some wrestling holds my brother taught me. All the big kids are going outside to the picnic table."

Corey obediently followed, until Jimmy came to a sudden stop at the hallway. "Do we get root beer floats?"

"Of course," I said. "Go get some from Keith."

The boys detoured into the kitchen while I desperately hoped no one else thought this was a party. Lindsi was dressed to kill in a short red skirt and matching vest, but Lindsi was always dressed to kill.

"It's lucky it's sunny out and not raining today." After that got out of my mouth, I noticed I was standing there patting my fingers together. I dropped my arms to my sides and silently led the girls into our backyard.

Keith and Lindsi had the table set with glasses of root beer floats on pink napkins. It almost did look like a party.

"I take it you're Marybelle," Keith said to her. "Sit on this side between me and Jason. Lindsi, you can sit on the other side of me."

While Marybelle walked around the table, Keith pointed to Susan and Crystal. "You two girls sit across from us with Gretchen."

Everyone dutifully took the appointed seats, except Keith, who remained standing above us. "The game we're going to play is called 'True stories.' I'll call the name of the first storyteller, and that person has to tell about the subject I assign them. Nobody else can interrupt the storyteller, but everyone will have a turn. Got it?"

"What's the point?" Lindsi asked. You aren't dumb when you get all the A's in school Lindsi gets.

"Nobody is supposed to know the point until the end of the game. Our little group here is going to solve a mystery."

Luckily, Lindsi believed this, or at least she shut up.

"Let's see." Keith stroked his chin, pretending to be thinking. "Let's see. Gretchen, you know the game, so you be the first storyteller. Hmmm." More stroking of his chin. "How about telling the true story of the blue earrings?"

I didn't look to the left or the right or across the table, but kept my eyes on Keith. I started the story with Marybelle telling me about Susan shoplifting the earrings and ended the story with Lindsi yelling at Susan for borrowing them.

When I finished, I dared to look at Marybelle. She was shrugging her shoulders casually. "So I just made a mistake and thought I saw Susan and . . ."

"No, no," Keith interrupted her. "You can't say anything until it's your turn to be the storyteller. Then everybody will listen to you."

Marybelle placed both her hands on the table. For a second I thought that she was going to leave. Instead, she looked back at me with her green eyes glittering.

She would wait to tell her story all right, but none of it would be true. Keith's plan was going to be a total bust.

"Crystal," Keith said, "you be next. You tell the true story of the kiss in the classroom."

Crystal looked confused. She's not the smartest thing around. "But it turned out Ms. Cooper's going to marry Mr. Herbert."

"That's fine," Keith said, "but that's the end of the story. Be a storyteller and start at the beginning when you first thought the principal kissed your teacher."

"Oh, that's only what Marybelle said."

Keith leaned forward as if he were talking to a five-year-old. "And when did Marybelle tell you this and where were you when she told you?"

Crystal managed a jumbled version of Marybelle walking us around the playground, telling us she saw Mr. Swenson kiss Ms. Cooper.

"Now," Keith said. "Now it's your turn, Susan. Tell the true story of what Marybelle said Gretchen did."

Susan's eyes flew open wide, but she didn't say a word.

Lindsi said, "Go ahead, Susan. What have you got to lose?"

Susan still didn't say a word. We were old, old friends and I knew she didn't want to tell on me.

Lindsi nodded at her. I was thinking maybe Lindsi had caught on to the game.

"Come on, Susan," she coaxed. "Tell what Marybelle said about Gretchen. Gretchen deserves to know."

Susan thought about that a minute and then started her story slowly. "One Monday after school Marybelle came to our house. She said her mother thought she should talk to me and my mom about Gretchen. We all sat down on the couch, and Marybelle told us that Gretchen had been stealing things from their house.

She'd stolen expensive hair-cutting scissors from her mom's perm kit. Marybelle's mom caught her with them in her pocket. Mrs. Jackson told Gretchen she could never come in their house again. And Mrs. Jackson thought we should know, so Gretchen wouldn't steal from us."

"Susan, you can't believe this," I begged. "Why would I want scissors?"

Keith reminded me with a jerk of his head that we were in the middle of a game.

I closed my mouth.

"And now Marybelle." He looked down at the little liar. "It's your turn to tell the true story."

"All right," Marybelle said. Calmly, she retold everyone's story, apologizing sweetly for mistaking Mr. Swenson for Mr. Herbert. She ended with no apologies to me, because her mother had caught me stealing.

She sounded perfectly reasonable. Anyone would believe her.

CHAPTER 17

The Clicked-on Brain

❦ "Marybelle," Keith asked, "when did your mom catch Gretchen stealing?"

"Let's see. It was the Sunday before she was absent. I remember perfectly, because I thought Gretchen was too ashamed to show up on Monday. And then after school, I walked over to Susan's house to warn her." Marybelle passed around a queenly smile to everyone but me. She knew she had won.

I was picturing her face squashed in a headlock when my brain clicked on.

"Wait a minute! Wait a minute!" I waved my arms wildly. Crystal ducked and Susan cringed away from me.

"Wait *just* a minute." I was in control now, with my hand pointing at a startled Marybelle. "That was the Sunday my dad and I got poisoned by the rug chemicals. Mom made us go to her house. We were there all day. And we stayed all night. And the next day, Mom and I went shopping."

"Oh. Oh." I could almost see the gears shift behind Marybelle's green eyes. "I must have been mistaken about which day it was. Let's see . . ."

Lindsi leaned around Keith to face Marybelle. "You don't make mistakes, you little liar. And you're so good at lying, my mother believed you!"

Marybelle tried to shrug this off, but her mouth had begun to quiver at the corners. And what happened next was something I never expected to see. Never, never thought I'd see.

Marybelle's head drooped, and fat round tears plopped onto the pink napkin below her face. We all sat like frozen dummies, watching Marybelle's bowed head as she cried silently, letting tear after tear drop from her eyes.

"I want to go home," she whispered. "Please call Corey, so we can go home."

Jason started to get up from the table.

"No, wait another minute," I told him. "I want to know why she did it. I never did anything to you, Marybelle. Ever."

Marybelle sucked in a long breath. "You wouldn't be my friend. I was just trying to get a friend."

"You were trying to get a friend by killing off the competition?" Keith asked.

"You could have tried to be nice," Crystal said primly.

"I did." Marybelle wiped a hand across her face. "I tried to be nice to you, Crystal."

"You weren't nice to me, Marybelle," Susan said. "You cut my hair on purpose."

"But you wear such pretty clothes."

"Pretty clothes!" Susan exclaimed. "Mom and Lindsi like pretty clothes. You try to slide to first base without tearing your *pretty* clothes. Spider always picks Gretchen to play ball, but nobody picks me."

"Oh, tough, teacher's pet." Marybelle's voice was bitter. "If you get one thing dirty, you've got ten other outfits to put on. And your precious friend, Gretchen, gets presents, and her little brother gets presents. And my little brother gets nothing! *Nothing!*"

Marybelle's eyes flooded with tears again. "Please," she pleaded to Jason. "I want to go home."

Jason ran into the house. When he came back, he had Dad, Corey, and Jimmy with him. As soon as Corey saw Marybelle, he stopped to search each of our faces. "What happened? What did you do to my sister?"

No one answered him and he scurried around the table. "What happened, Marybelle? Did they hurt you?"

She shook her head no.

Corey placed his small hand against her wet cheek and gently turned her head so he could peer into her teary eyes. "Are you sure?" he asked her. "Are you sure they didn't hurt you?"

It was hurting me to watch his worried little face. It must have upset Jason, too, because he moved around the picnic table and helped Marybelle to her feet. "Come on, Corey," Jason said. "We'll take her home."

I turned around on the bench to watch them leave. Dad led the way while Jason walked on one side of Marybelle. Corey stayed close to her other side, keeping a tight hold on her hand.

Not one of us at the table spoke until the sound of Dad's car faded away.

"Did you order the food?" Keith asked me.

"The food? Yes, yes. But I told them I'd call back when we were almost ready."

I stayed inside until the pizza truck came. I didn't feel like talking to anyone. It took all of my silver dollars and some of my paper dollars to pay the delivery man. I lugged out the pizza boxes and told Keith he could bring out the cake.

Lindsi went with him for a knife and more napkins. She was cutting the pizza when Dad and Jason returned. "Do I get some, too?" Dad asked.

"Of course," Lindsi said. "You get the biggest piece."

Dad sat down next to me. I was glad to have him there and leaned my head against his shoulder. I'd expected to be relieved when all Marybelle's lies were exposed, but instead I was sick about the whole thing.

I looked across the table at Jason. He didn't seem wimpy to me anymore. Just miserable and lost. A skinny leftover in the family. Not the big brother. Not the cute little brother. Not the only girl. I didn't know anything about Jason's school life, but the guys probably crossed him off as fast as I always had.

"Jason," Lindsi said. "You want some with Canadian bacon?"

"Naw," Jason said. "I don't feel hungry. I feel sorry for that girl with no friends."

"You should feel sorry for your sister," Crystal told him. "Because of Marybelle's lies, Gretchen was never going to be allowed in our houses."

"Gretchen can always go someplace else," he said.

"She won't need to now," Crystal said. "Now we'll all eat lunch together again. Right, Gretchen?"

"Maybe sometimes," I said. "But I like reading books with Amy."

Susan's face crumpled. "Gretchen, I'm really, really sorry I believed you'd stolen things at Marybelle's house."

"That's okay. Sometimes I thought you'd shoplifted the blue earrings. But what I don't get is, if your Mom's so smart, why did she believe Marybelle's story?"

"Oh, that," Lindsi said. "You remember one day when you were looking at Mom's letter opener and I told you to put it back down on her desk? Well, after that, Mom couldn't find the letter opener."

"I was just looking at it, because I thought the jewels in the handle were pretty. What would I do with a letter opener? The only thing I get in the mail is birthday cards from my dentist and my grandma. I've been in your house for five years and you think I'm a thief."

"No, we don't. No, we don't," Susan cried. "Any of

Mom's customers could have taken the letter opener. It was just that when Marybelle told us the lie, Lindsi reminded Mom about the missing letter opener."

"Nice touch," Keith said to Lindsi.

"Who knew then?" Lindsi shot back. "Marybelle's a good storyteller."

"I know what Marybelle is," Jimmy announced. "She's a liar."

"Maybe she is." Jason's face drooped with sadness. "But it isn't easy for some people to figure out how to get a friend. Who's going to help her now?"

"If the music teacher sees her feeling bad, he will," I said.

But, I wondered, who would help Jason?

Dad stood up and brushed cake crumbs off his pants. "You kids clean up the mess."

"We will," Lindsi said. "Jason, you get the glasses and Jimmy, you take the knife off the table."

Jason and Jimmy dutifully collected the knife and glasses and took them in the house.

"Now, Keith, get the garbage can."

Keith did, and Lindsi swooped everything left into the can.

"Done!" she said proudly and looked up for approval from Keith.

He took her arm to walk her to the front yard. The rest of us trailed behind them.

"See you tomorrow at school?" Susan asked after she got on her bike.

I didn't want her feelings to be hurt when I ate with Amy, so I chose my answer carefully. "Sure," I said, "I'll save you a seat on the bus in the morning."

After the girls were gone, I teased Keith. "Lindsi tried hard enough to impress you."

"Lindsi's too fancy for me," he said. "I want Angela. She has a golden heart."

I didn't ask if she had wings, too. I reached up and hugged him. I'd never hugged him before in my life. "You turned out to be a neat big brother."

"What about me?" Jimmy asked.

I stooped down to give him a hug, and then I stepped toward Jason. He stiffened with surprise, but he managed a little awkward hug back.

CHAPTER 18

Big, Fat, and Wide

🍂 For the next two weeks at school, Marybelle ate her lunch by herself. She took a little bite after a little bite from her sandwiches, keeping her eyes focused on her desk.

"She looks shriveled," Amy said. She said this even after I'd told her about the lying game.

"Marybelle should be," I said. "She had me banned from all my friends' houses."

"Yes, but she looks so sad."

"Liars aren't supposed to be happy when they're caught. What is this? Blame the victim and be sorry for the criminal?"

Amy shook her head. "I don't blame you. I wouldn't like it if someone told lies about me."

"No, but I bet you drag home stray cats," I said.

Amy laughed. "I can't. My mom has three bird-houses."

Ms. Cooper was spending too much time gazing at

her engagement ring to check out Marybelle, but of course Mr. Monte did. I'd expected him to notice how Marybelle slumped in her seat, barely singing and never shouting out questions or putting down Robbie. I expected Mr. Monte to keep her after music class to find out what was bothering her. I'd hoped she wouldn't peddle any of her lies and make me look bad. But I was shook by what he really did.

First he announced that Ms. Cooper had chosen the fourth day of June for her wedding and was inviting the seven entertainers to take part in the ceremony. She especially wanted Robbie to sing "The Tennessee Waltz" again. Then Mr. Monte said he thought the group would need a piano player, too.

He looked over his glasses at Marybelle. "Marybelle," he said, "I think I could teach you to be an accompanist."

"Teach her two whole songs in a month?" Robbie asked.

"Maybe not the melody, but she could learn the chords. How about it, Marybelle? Would you give up your lunch hour and come in here and practice with me for four weeks?"

Dumb question. Of course Marybelle agreed to take her sandwiches into the music room.

I complained about this to Susan and Jason. "Mr. Monte never offered to teach anyone else the piano. I could have played the piano and sung. Marybelle's completely rotten and then she sits around looking abused, and everybody feels sorry for her because she's poor, and nobody thinks of what she did."

"Yeah, but you can figure out how to get along, and it isn't so easy for other people," Jason said.

"I figure things out because I try one thing and if it doesn't work, I try something else. Marybelle just tells lie after lie."

"True," Susan said.

We three were sitting around my living room the weekend before the wedding. Jason had his legs stretched out in front of his chair the way Keith does. But he'd had to scoot his bottom forward to get the same long-legged effect.

"Maybe I should have my hair cut short and permed before next Sunday," I suggested.

"Don't do that," Jason said. "Weave your hair together and tie it up on your head. That looks classy."

Susan nodded. "A French braid does look classy on you, Gretchen. Jason's right."

A pleased smile popped on Jason's face, which he quickly hid with the back of his hand. I almost made a crack about Mr. Cool, but I didn't. I remembered Jason hadn't whined once since I'd started treating him like a human being.

"I wonder what Marybelle will wear to the wedding," I said.

"Probably her old jeans," Susan said.

"She can't," I said. "Mr. Monte wants the girls to

wear dresses and the boys to wear white shirts."

"What are you going to wear?" Susan asked.

"I don't know yet. Mom's taking me shopping next Saturday."

"Maybe that Marybelle could get a dress at the Salvation Army," Jason said. "That's where we drop off our pants when they get too short. A dress there would probably only cost five dollars."

Susan wasn't interested in what Marybelle would wear to the wedding. She wanted to complain about being left out. "I don't see why Ms. Cooper didn't invite the whole class."

"Probably because the caterer's bill would break her bank account," Jason said.

But it didn't matter how much we complained. Susan wasn't going to the wedding, and Marybelle was going to play the piano.

She was there for all the entertainers' rehearsals. After our songs were sung, we had to stand quietly in a row while Marybelle thumped out the wedding march.

Spider stood beside me, and he wasn't quiet at our last rehearsal. In time with Marybelle's chords, he sang under his breath, "Here comes the bride, big, fat, and wide. See how she waa-ddles from si-ide to side."

I couldn't muffle my giggles, and Mr. Monte shook his head at us. When we left the music room, I warned Spider, "Don't you dare make me laugh during the wedding."

Keith had turned sixteen in May. He offered to drive me to the church, but Dad said he didn't want to endanger more than one of our lives at a time.

"Maybe," I said to Dad as we rode along, "Keith might turn out to be a good driver. He isn't such a bully anymore. He helped me and he takes care of Jimmy."

After I said that, I remembered Keith had always taken care of Jimmy. I shook my head. "It's funny, but since the trouble with Marybelle, it seems like I'm looking through a kaleidoscope."

"How's that?" Dad asked.

. "Well, everything keeps shifting. I always thought Jason was a crybaby, but when he was sorry for Marybelle, he only seemed lonesome. And I always thought Susan was the greatest. I still like her, but Amy makes up her own mind. Even about me."

I looked at Dad, who had pulled up in front of the church. "Do you know what I mean?"

"I know." He leaned over to give me a good-bye kiss on my cheek.

Masaka was waiting at the entrance of the church. We went through the door together. Inside, we tried to poke our way past clusters of people in their best clothes, greeting each other. An usher came up and asked us if we were friends of the bride or groom.

"We're part of the entertainment," I told him.

He pointed to the last aisle, where we found the rest of the singers with Mr. Monte. "It's about time," Robbie said.

While Mr. Monte herded us down the aisle, Spider gave me a once-over. My hair was in a French braid. I wore a sleeveless rose-colored dress with a Mandarin collar. Mom said it made me look exotic. Spider said, "You look pretty good."

I could feel myself blush.

The piano was placed to the far left side of the altar. Marybelle was already sitting on the piano stool. She was wearing a sky blue dress and at first I thought she looked pretty good, too. Then, as Mr. Monte lined us up behind her, I noticed the shoulders of her dress sagged down her arms. Maybe a dress two sizes too big was all she could find at the Salvation Army.

I looked down at my cream-colored shoes with the little heels. Next I glanced at Marybelle's feet, which were tucked under the piano. A pang went through my heart when I saw she was wearing her old, dirty running shoes. Jason was right, I thought. It couldn't be easy being Marybelle.

But she sat up tall anyway, and after all the people had settled in the pews, she played the first chords of "The Tennessee Waltz." Robbie stepped forward and his silvery voice rang through the church.

We followed Robbie's solo with "Beautiful Dreamer," and after a pause, Marybelle began the wedding march. I waited for a thin, nervous Ms. Cooper to appear. Instead, a radiant Ms. Cooper in a white lace gown stepped down the aisle.

Masaka gasped, "A princess!"

I turned to look at Spider. His mouth was hanging open. Without thinking, I reached up to close it. He grabbed my hand and held it for a minute before he let it go.